About the
Black Clouds

Book Three

The Tale of Many Worlds

E. L. Mendell

Book Seven

About the Black Clouds
Book three, The Tale of Many Worlds
By E. L. Mendell
Copyright ©2022
Rewrite 2026
All rights reserved.

Snow Dragon Publishing
Shelby, OH. 44875
First Printing 2026
Cover art by Abigail Mendell
Printed on acid-free paper

Library of Congress Control No: 202294445
ISBN: 978-1-950218-97-4

Snow Dragon 2026

This one is for those toxic friends
who I had to cut out of my life.
I hope you're each doing well.

Table of Contents

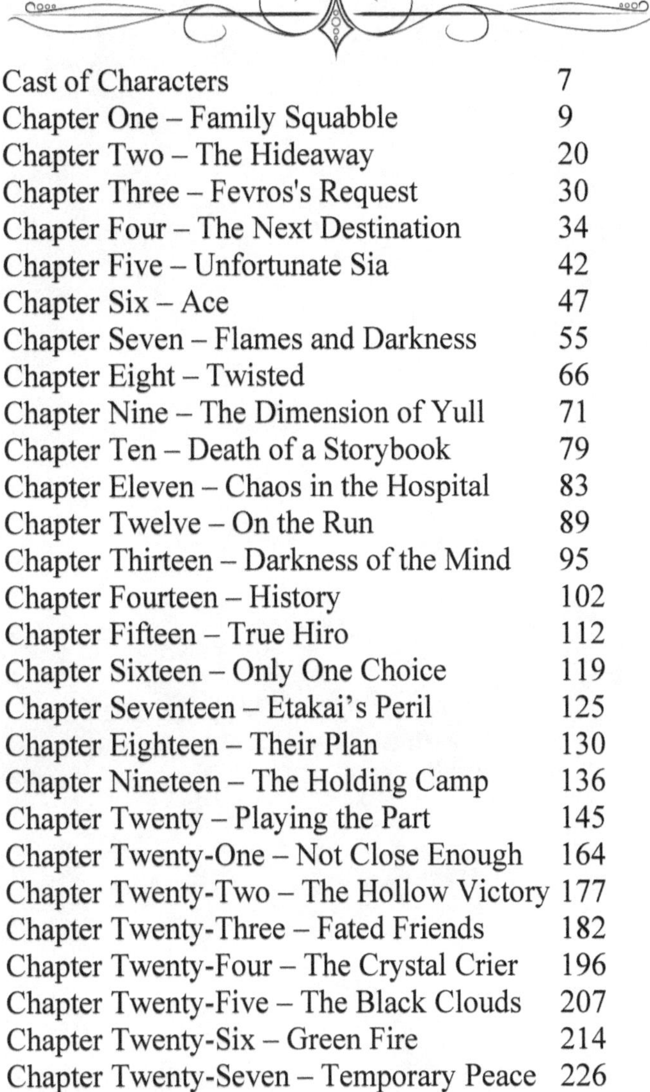

Book Seven

Cast of Characters

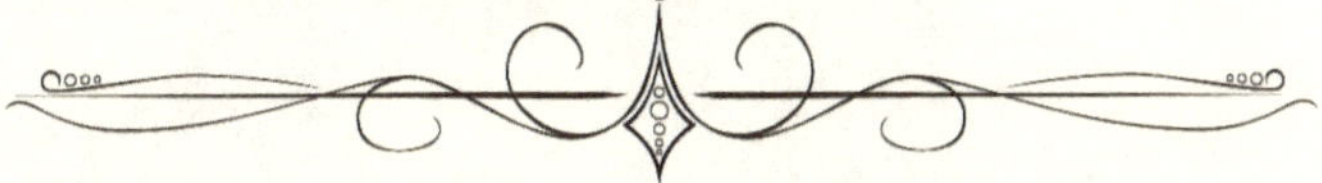

Etakai
(*eh-tah-ka-ee*)

Reitrin
(*ray-trin*)

Shan Kaffie
(*sh-ahn*) (*ka-fee*)

Sia
(*see-ah*)

Fevros
(*fev-ross*)

Aoiro
(*ah-oy-ee-row*)

Hiro
(*hee-row*)

Gechio
(*ge-chee-oh*)

Book Seven

Chapter One
Family Squabble

Shadows covered the walls. It was so cold the furnace kicked on. Reitrin held the blankets up to her nose, gazing at the ceiling. A red glow from her clock came from the desk beside her. It told her it was four o'clock in the morning, but it could have been wrong. She had reset it after unplugging it to use as a weapon the night before when Etakai entered the house unannounced.

There was something moving in the other room. She hadn't heard the door of the spare bedroom open, so it couldn't have been Shan, her friend whose restaurant had burned down that night. If Shan were even awake he would have probably remained in bed too. He had a lot of injuries and would not try to be a hero.

Something clattered in the kitchen and Reitrin jumped. It couldn't have been Etakai. He was much too quiet and graceful to drop anything while sneaking around.

Reitrin rolled out of bed and unplugged her clock.

If Etakai wasn't going to deal with the intruder then she would have to. Reitrin wondered where Etakai was. He liked to play hero. What if it was him making the noise? Reitrin would scold him then return to bed. But, what if it was a real intruder?

Reitrin's heart was racing. If there was trouble would Etakai come to her rescue? In the story he came from, he was the hero. But since being left in the Real World he was not the most agreeable person. He and Reitrin did not get along.

It felt like he had been a curse in her life for ages, but it had only been two days in the Real World. The day before, Reitrin had been stuck in a book called *The Lord of Desolation*. Etakai had been in the story also, but she had not seen him until their last hours in the story. Then they were sent out of the book.

Reitrin knew days had passed in the book, but when they returned to the Real World it was only minutes.

With her stress levels skyrocketing, Reitrin trembled as she placed her hand on the knob. But still she hesitated.

Was it a monster like the ones in *The Lord of Desolation*; the creature that climbed the cliffs? Was it one of the book jumpers called Eysheus? Or maybe it was some other storybook character that had been dragged out of their pages and found its way into her kitchen?

It could have been anything.

Reitrin readied her clock and pushed open the door.

The lights were on. The fridge was open. From over top the island Reitrin saw a blonde head with braided hair and a lace top with a black strapless shirt underneath.

"You!" Reitrin yelled, lowering the clock.

The woman in the fridge lifted her head and watched Reitrin with bored green eyes and a cookie in her mouth.

"Hey," said the woman, straightening up and

shutting the fridge. "Dad didn't restock his beer."

Reitrin glared daggers at the woman. There was a stench of stale wine in the air. Why hadn't she smelled that before? She would have known right away who had entered the apartment by the scent.

"What are you doing here, Sia?" Reitrin demanded. "You gave me a heart attack."

"I came to spend some time with you guys," replied Sia as she leaned on the counter and ate the cookie. "I mean, the sky is dark and stuff." She said this while waving to the giant window that overlooked the city. The apartment was on the third floor of the Cozy Castroph apartment complex. It had a lovely view of the city lights.

Reitrin glared out the window. "The black clouds are over the next town too?"

"Some friends and I tried driving to see where they ended," Sia said, finishing the cookie and dusting the crumbs off her fingers. "We never found a breaking point. They seem endless. What are they?"

"I don't know,"

"No need to be so snappy," muttered Sia, pushing back her blonde hair and leaving the kitchen. "Is dad asleep?"

"No," replied Reitrin.

"At work?"

"He's missing." Reitrin clenched her fists. "He's been missing for two days now."

Sia raised her thin eyebrows. "And when were you going to tell me?"

"I was sure he would show up before you ever thought of visiting again." Reitrin was glaring. "You never come here unless you need something, Sia. So, cut to the chase. What is it this time?”

“I told you,” replied Sia, an icy glare crossing her lovely features. “I wanted to spend time with you guys since the television reporters are saying this is the end of the world.”

Reitrin rolled her eyes. “Out of money again?”

Sia threw her arms in the air and turned away. She wore jeans, tall boots, and a lot of jewelry. The woman was a fashion diva to her friends and tried to keep up on latest trends by mooching off them. How she managed was beyond Reitrin.

Perhaps, to people unrelated to her, Sia was some kind of wonderful person? This was something Reitrin would never understand.

“I’ll use Dad’s room since he’s missing,” said Sia as she crossed the room and grabbed her bags. They were two large travel bags that could have fit Reitrin’s entire wardrobe.

“I wouldn’t do that if I were you,” said Reitrin as she watched her sister go to the other room.

“Oh, why is that?” Sia asked, giving her little sister a cold look. “Housing fugitives?”

“Sort of,” replied Reitrin under her breath. She leaned on the couch to watch and Sia raised an eyebrow. She shrugged, pushed open the door, and turned on the light.

For a moment she stood staring at the tall man inside the room.

His eyes glowed: the right was blue while the left was green and had black fangs tattooed underneath. His silvery hair was messed up and he wore only the pajama pants Reitrin had lent him.

Sia was too alarmed to scream. She fell on her

rear, pointing at him and struggling to find words.

"Who is this?" Etakai asked, locking Reitrin in his stare.

"Etakai, meet my older sister," said Reitrin motioning to Sia who was opening and closing her mouth like a fish out of water. "Her name is Sia. I'd be careful if I was you, she has a habit of falling madly in love with handsome men." Reitrin knew warning Etakai was useless. She saw her sister was already starting to realize how handsome Etakai was.

Nothing would save him from her flirtatious nature now.

"And you believe me to be in danger of this?" Etakai asked. "Is that a complement?"

"Your writer did a good job with you," replied Reitrin. "I'm not trying to flatter you. It's what anyone would expect from a storybook hero. Is Shan still asleep?"

"Like the dead," replied Etakai, looking over his shoulder. He turned off the light. "When I heard the front door unlock I hid in here. He didn't move so I checked his pulse. He's alive, but I didn't realize a human could sleep as deep as he is."

"Well, his body is recovering from a lot," muttered Reitrin. She glanced at Sia who was gawking at Etakai, still opening and closing her mouth as if trying to figure out what to say. Reitrin saw the blush on Sia's face and rolled her eyes. Yes, Sia was already captivated by Etakai. Reitrin shrugged hopelessly and went to her bedroom.

"And now you're leaving?" Etakai shot. "I refuse to deal with this."

"Then sleep on the floor in Shan's room," said

Reitrin as she entered her room. "There's a lock on the door and Sia knows where the couch is." She then locked herself in her bedroom and released a long breath.

That had been too much drama for so early in the morning.

Shaking her head, Reitrin took her clock and plugged it back into the wall. She would adjust the time later. She went to the small window beside her bed and pushed aside the dark curtains.

Reitrin gazed at the black clouds sadly. Were people really saying it was the end of the world?

Sia banged on the door. Reitrin roll her eyes.

"What?" She called, crossing the room.

"I'll take your room," Sia called through the wood. "It isn't dignified for a lady to sleep on the couch."

"What am I then, a poodle?"

"You may as well be."

Reitrin cursed her sister's name. "I'm too tired for this. You show up at an ungodly hour and expect pampering? Go get a hotel, mooch."

"This is a hotel!"

"This is an apartment that our father rented for *two* people," Reitrin argued. "And last I heard he told you to pay rent when you come to visit."

"That was an empty threat–"

"Enough!"

Reitrin jumped back when Etakai kicked open her door, which crashed against the wall.

"If I have to burn down the apartment to shut you two up I will!" Etakai roared, making the women stare in horror. "I don't often sleep well, but when I do I expect to be disturbed only by sunrise or impending doom. Neither of which are you. Now shut the hell up or get out!" He went back to the other room and slammed the door shut.

Reitrin and Sia stood in an awkward silence.

"He broke the doorknob," Sia whispered, looking at the splintered wood.

Reitrin buried her face in her hands, but then went to her bed and removed her pillow and comforter.

"Get in there and don't bother me again," she growled, walking past her sister who skipped into the bedroom and attempted to shut the broken door.

Reitrin collapsed on the couch. "Why do I keep collecting unwelcome guests?"

She wondered what her sister wanted. Sia only ever brought trouble when she came to visit. Asking for money or temporary lodging while the friend she mooched off of was between homes. Her life had always sounded like chaos to Reitrin. Their dad cared for Sia's well being though. Harold Nichol would treat Sia like a daughter, and Reitrin was envious of this.

To Harold, Reitrin was just a murderer.

"Whatever," Reitrin grumbled. She rolled over and pulled the blankets over her head. There was no hope of sleeping well that night.

She woke up to Sia leaving the bedroom and knocking on the wood of the couch.

"What's for breakfast?" Sia asked.

"Your heart on a platter," Reitrin grumbled. She rolled over and got off the couch. She went to her room to get dressed and remained in the bathroom until she was calm enough to deal with Sia.

Reitrin now had three guests in her apartment. An apartment meant only for two. What would she do to house them all? Reitrin rubbed her face with a frustrated groan. Her life was chaos. She left the bathroom and found her bed covers jumbled and Sia's clothes on the floor.

Sia always left a mess wherever she went. Reitrin wouldn't have been surprised if the woman had finally got on her friends nerves and was kicked out.

That would explain her unexpected visit.

In the kitchen, Sia was looking through the fridge again.

"I'm making coffee," she said to Reitrin. "I made enough for all of us."

Reitrin raised her eyebrows. "Okay, what are you after? You never do anything for others."

Sia shut the fridge and gave Reitrin a cold look. "You think so little of me."

"Is that surprising? Just what have you ever done for dad and me?"

Sia looked away without reply.

Reitrin scoffed and reached past her, grabbing a granola bar from the counter. She fetched a coffee cup from the strainer and tapped the water off the bottom.

"I don't have a place to stay right now," said Sia quietly.

"No?"

Sia shook her head. "My friend was evicted because he hadn't been paying rent, so I'm going to be here while I wait for him to call me and tell me he has a new place."

"Why not find someone else to babysit you?" Reitrin muttered, pouring the coffee.

Sia scowled.

The spare bedroom door opened and both girls shut up.

Etakai stepped out, pushing back his silvery hair and giving them an annoyed look. He had forgotten there was a new nuisance.

"Hello, handsome," said Sia, looking Etakai up and down.

Etakai gave her a disgusted look and turned to Reitrin. "Shan is finally awake and getting washed up. He seems okay, but he's in a daze."

"Everyone is acting weird today," replied Reitrin, arching an eyebrow. "Sia made coffee for us and Shan isn't talking. Are you going to start acting nice?"

"Not likely," replied Etakai.

"You drink coffee, right?" Sia eyed Etakai expectantly.

"No." Etakai left them and went to the large bay window the overlooked the city.

Reitrin rolled her eyes. It made sense now. Sia had made the coffee in hopes of impressing Etakai.

"When did Dad go missing again?" Sia asked, fiddling with her hair, which Reitrin noticed had been freshly brushed and tied up. She was trying to be pretty for Etakai.

Reitrin snorted into her coffee and Sia gave her a confused look.

"What was that?" Sia snapped.

"Just thought of something funny," Reitrin murmured into the mug. She shook her head. "We think dad was kidnapped. I came home two nights ago and found the apartment was a mess. Dad was gone. It looked as if he hadn't had time to set any of his things down before they took him."

"And you didn't tell me?"

"I haven't reported it to the police yet either." Reitrin was thankful Shan happened to step out of the bedroom just then, adjusting his sleeves and looking weary.

His nose was swollen. It had broken when a candle holder hit him. That had happened when a fight broke out in his restaurant and it burned to the ground afterwards. Reitrin couldn't blame him for looking distressed as he gazed around the room at everyone.

"Good morning. Did you all sleep well?" He gave Sia a puzzled look. "And you." His brow furrowed as he tried to figure out who she was.

"Did you hear nothing of what happened last night?" Reitrin asked.

Shan shook his head. "I slept well. Though not as well as I would have liked." He frowned, his gaze drifting away as if he was going to another world in his mind.

"Do you want coffee?" Reitrin asked.

Shan snapped out of his daze and shook his head. "How about we all get breakfast at the local diner?" He suggested. "It will be my treat. I don't feel right taking anything from an employee. A room for sleep is already too much."

"You spent the night in my father's bedroom because your home is gone," said Reitrin. "It's okay." She looked towards Etakai who was watching them over his shoulder.

"I could use some breakfast," said Sia, raising her hand excitedly.

"You'll pay for your own," Reitrin growled.

"What?" Sia barked.

"Its okay, Reitrin," said Shan. "Come on, let's go. It's not a far walk. I have a lot to discuss with you guys." He looked to Etakai who heaved a sigh.

"I'll escort you. But that's all."

"Good enough," said Shan. And for the first time since his restaurant burned down, a smile touched his face.

Chapter Two
The Hideaway

"I really wish you hadn't broken my bedroom door," Reitrin said as she pulled up her collar against the wind. She had told Shan all of what happened the night before as they walked down the street. A cold morning wind was blowing and the black clouds swirled above their heads.

"It's repairable," muttered Etakai.

"Did I really sleep through all that?" Shan blew on his cold hands and laughed. "I had no idea I slept so deep."

"I was having a hard time figuring out who was in the apartment," said Reitrin, shaking her head. "I would have never guessed it was my sister." She glanced back at Sia who was trailing behind them, playing with her cell phone.

"I can't believe you two think you're related," grumbled Etakai, glaring over his shoulder at Sia.

"We are related," said Reitrin. "Sadly. In the Real World we can't choose our siblings."

"I disagree with you," said Etakai.

"Am I surprised?" Reitrin muttered under her breath. "No. Not at all."

"Your sister is nothing like you."

"I know. We've never liked each other. Not since out mother died."

"Are you sure you're really sisters?"

Reitrin scowled. "I wish it weren't true."

Etakai gazed across the dark streets. It felt cold

that morning and he wondered if the clouds were thickening and making it harder for the sunlight to warm the earth.

"We have to walk past the next two blocks," said Shan, pointing ahead. "Then take a left, and it will be around the corner."

"I'll drop you two off," said Etakai. "There's somewhere I need to go."

"Where is that?" Reitrin asked.

"The library."

"Why?" Reitrin gave him a suspicious look.

"I just want to make sure Garvon's story wasn't returned to the shelf last night."

"Oh." Reitrin frowned and looked away. She had not forgotten Garvon, the king with long white hair who had shown up half dead in Shan's restaurant the day before. Chief, the leader of the Secret Police, had taken Garvon's book during the chaotic events.

Reitrin shivered when she remembered the Secret Police and their eerie members. The dangers they mentioned and the warning that they were watching her, Etakai, and Shan. Their Chief had told them that, if they ever entered another storybook, the three of them would be arrested. This made Reitrin shiver. She didn't like the thought of being arrested by someone who may or may not even be a part of the Real World. After all, the Chief had mentioned that book jumpers had been causing problems for years.

How many years, no one had said, but they did say the book jumpers called Eysheus were the only ones that could cause real damage.

"There," said Shan as they rounded the bend and came down a new street where many cars were parked along the sidewalk. The streetlights flickered and a sign with "Lana's Diner" written on it was creaking in the wind. It was eerie, but the diner looked chipper and bright.

There was a "welcome" sign over the "open" sign and the hours underneath that. Music could be heard coming from inside and Shan led the way to the steps.

"Please join us, Etakai," said Shan as he stopped outside the wooden door. Through the windows, which were crammed full of antique toys and artifacts, the inside was colorful with square tables and tile flooring.

"Not very tasteful," said Etakai, peering past him.

"I love this place," said Sia, looking up from her phone. "They have the best pancakes!" She hurried past the others and went inside.

Reitrin peered in through the glass to see Sia take a seat at the counter where the bar stools spun.

"Please," Shan said again to Etakai. "I have some business I'd like to discuss with you and Reitrin."

"Business?" Reitrin asked.

"Yes," replied Shan. "My restaurant burned down last night, but I got an idea from it and I'd like to know what you two think. So please, come inside too."

Etakai rolled his eyes, but did not argue as Shan led him and Reitrin into the diner.

There was old dance music playing in the background and a television showing the news, which Sia was watching as she swirled her lemon water with a straw. The woman behind the bar was older with curly gray hair. Her glasses were perched on her nose and she looked over the rims at them as they entered.

"What'll you have?" She called over the music.

"Coffee," said Shan as he joined Sia at the counter. He had a moment of difficulty, trying to get on the stool with all his injuries. Reitrin took his arm and helped him. He was pale when he thanked her.

Reitrin sat beside him, and Etakai took the vacant seat by hers. He eyed everything with disdain.

"Water?" The waitress asked, looking from Etakai to Reitrin. "Coffee? Or perhaps tea or soda?"

"I'll have coffee," said Reitrin.

"Hot tea," muttered Etakai, staring at the television. "Unsweetened."

The waitress nodded and left to get the drinks.

"What is it?" Reitrin asked, noticing Etakai's blank expression.

"The black clouds," said Etakai, nodding to the television. "Look, that flying machine is trying to follow them to find their end."

Reitrin watched as the reporter on the helicopter spoke over the wind, though the television was muted so they couldn't hear him. The subtitles underneath showed he spoke of the black clouds as a strange phenomenon and said they were not made of liquid and scientists were trying to find out what they really were, but they could not collect samples because the clouds avoided them.

"The clouds avoid them?" Shan frowned. "How can a cloud avoid anything?"

"I wonder what they are," said Reitrin as their drinks arrived. "Could it be a type of gas?"

"If it were gas it wouldn't have a mind of its own

like these clouds seem to," Shan murmured. "How strange."

"Cream and sugar," said the waitress, setting them in front of Reitrin. "Now, what can I do you guys for?"

Etakai gave the woman a bewildered stare.

"She wants to know what you're eating," said Reitrin, passing Etakai a menu.

"I'm not hungry," said Etakai at once, and he looked back at the news.

Reitrin, Shan and Sia placed their orders and as soon as the waitress was gone Shan turned to Reitrin. "I am going to open a new restaurant."

"What?" Reitrin was surprised. "You just lost your old one yesterday."

"Working in a restaurant is my dream," Shan explained with a childish smile. "So I want a new start, and a new menu. I've actually been debating on changing things up for a while now, so this is the big start I needed."

"Maybe give the place a new name too," Reitrin suggested.

"What's wrong with Kaffie's Café?" Shan complained.

"The place wasn't a café," Reitrin replied. "The only coffee beverage you had was coffee with cream and sugar. A real café would have more coffee products and other drinks on the menu."

"I though café meant a small restaurant selling light meals and drinks," Shan said with confusion.

"That may be the definition," Reitrin replied. "But when people hear the name 'café' they expect lots of coffee, not Asian food."

"Are you from a storybook?" Etakai inquired.

"No," replied Shan, frowning at Etakai. "I was raised in another country for most of my life before I moved here. I learned to cook and speak this language in my later years, but some of the words continue to confuse me." He frowned at Reitrin who rubbed her face and glared at Etakai.

"You have to quit thinking everyone is from a storybook," she told him, glancing towards Sia to make sure her sister wasn't hearing any of this. Sia was playing on her phone, oblivious to the world.

"Anyone could be from a story," Etakai replied. "There are thousands of stories, and a thousand more characters in those stories. This entire city could be made of fictional characters and we'd never know it."

Reitrin gazed into her coffee with a frown. "I don't like thinking that way."

"Hideaway," said Shan, snapping his fingers.

Etakai and Reitrin gave him blank looks.

"Come again?" Reitrin asked.

"The Hideaway," replied Shan. "Twice now I've had storybook characters wander into my restaurant while injured and lost. What if we made a restaurant where fictional characters can come and be hidden from the Real World?"

"You're insane!" Reitrin burst. "Why would you encourage them?"

"Because this world can be awful when you're unfamiliar with it," said Shan, staring at Reitrin as if he had thought she would understand. "I had a hard life before I got that restaurant. Etakai wandered in there and found the help he needed. Garvon wandered in there because he was injured. Even you came there when you needed shelter. I think making it a haven for wandering characters, real and fictional, would be brilliant! That way they can go there when they grow sick of this world and its cruelties and find a place where they're accepted as they are."

"You wouldn't make much money off them," Etakai muttered into his teacup. "Most of them will be poor when they show up."

"That doesn't matter," said Shan. "If you and Reitrin are helping out I'm sure I'll be able to draw in business from real people too."

Etakai looked at Reitrin who was staring at the counter, lost in thought.

"I don't hate the idea," Etakai told Shan. "But you'll have a hard time explaining some of the freaks that'll walk in there."

"They won't need to be explained, that's what makes this idea so wonderful," said Shan.

The waitress returned with their food and the conversation died away. Reitrin ate waffles with applesauce and Shan dug into a colorful omelet. Sia was enjoying fluffy pancakes smothered in syrup. Etakai continued to watch the television.

"It's not a bad idea," muttered Etakai, making Reitrin glance at him.

"Are you still on the Hideaway idea?" Reitrin asked, wiping syrup off her lip.

Etakai nodded. "I wouldn't mind working in a place like that. We could get a lot of information from other characters that come and go. People have conversations in restaurants, like ours in this one." He motioned to the diner. "Neither of you stopped to think the waitress would hear us."

Reitrin and Shan looked up at the waitress who was washing dishes across the bar and pretended to not hear them.

"Oh," said Reitrin, felling embarrassed.

Etakai finished his tea and stood up. "I'm going to the library."

"I'll be going to the bank to get my finances in order," said Shan to Etakai. "We should all meet back at Reitrin's by noon at least."

Etakai nodded. "Watch your backs," he said as he left the counter. "This morning has been much too quiet."

"Maybe we'll make it through a day without ending up in a storybook?" Reitrin suggested.

Etakai stopped and gave her a blunt look. "Unlike you, I enjoy leaving this hellhole you call the Real World. I belong in the world of storybooks, not in this place." He strode past her and left the diner.

Reitrin watched him go with a frown. She wondered why it had never occurred to her that Etakai liked going into the storybooks. He was in his element when he found himself in a tale of good versus evil. She was the one who hated it. Even Shan seemed to embrace the storybook characters.

Then there was Sia, still eating and playing on her phone as if none of the strange conversation had happened beside her.

"Why am I the only one who thinks this is madness?" Reitrin asked, looking down at the last of the waffles.

"I don't see it as madness," said Shan. "I see it as a situation we need to make the best of. The Secret Police told us this has been going on for a long time.

These book jumpers have been causing problems for more people than just us, so I think it's something we need to take by the horns and learn to live with, especially since we're involved."

"Why are we involved?" Reitrin groaned.

Shan shrugged. "Can you escort me to the bank? I need to make sure my insurance holds up so we can start looking for a new building to turn into the Hideaway." Shan waved to the waitress. "Can I have the bill for all our meals?"

The waitress nodded and went to the back.

"You're leaving?" Sia asked, looking up when Reitrin slid off the stool.

"We have business to tend to," Reitrin explained. "I don't care what you do, as long as you don't mess around with anything in the apartment."

Sia scowled and turned back to her phone.

The waitress returned and Shan paid for the food, then he and Reitrin left the diner.

It was quiet. Cars drove by and Reitrin watched them pass with a grim gaze. How many fictional characters were running around the city? And how many had she encountered without knowing it? The thought made her uneasy.

"The bank is a bit further than I'd like to walk," said Shan. "Maybe we should look into getting a company car."

"I could borrow my dad's car if we need it," said Reitrin. "I have a spare key for it. I'm sure it's still in the garage since dad was kidnapped."

"Kidnapped?" Shan gave her a startled look. "What are you taking about?"

Reitrin sighed and ran her fingers through her

short brown hair. How had she forgotten? It hadn't been that long, but she had had no time to tell Shan about her father going missing.

She explained to him about when they returned from *Blood River*, she had found her apartment a mess and her father missing. She also told him about the red hair Etakai had found.

"Do you and Etakai know a redhead?" He asked as when they stopped at a crosswalk to wait for the light to change.

"Yes," replied Reitrin. "He is one of those … Eysheus, or whatever they're called. A book jumper."

Shan nodded slowly. "Well, we can't hate them if they're the ones bringing in our business."

The light turned and they crossed the street.

"I still think you're crazy," grumbled Reitrin.

"When life gives you lemons you make lemonade," said Shan thoughtfully. "It's the way the cards have fallen. I'm just jumping at the opportunity."

Reitrin sighed, but there was no more time to discuss it. They had arrived at the bank.

Chapter Three
Fevros's Request

Etakai arrived at the library as soon as it opened. The librarian greeted him with a smile before going to the front desk. She was a young girl with large glasses and her brown hair pulled back. Etakai only spared her a short look before rummaging the shelves where he had discovered *The Lord of Desolation*. The book was nowhere to be found.

He went to ask the librarian about the book and she informed him that it had been reported missing the day before.

"They really did take it," Etakai muttered, walking away. He found *Blood River* next and flipped through the pages. It felt hollow in his hands. He stopped and read a small portion; though figuring out each word took him a while. He had not learned much about reading. What he did know he had learned a long time ago.

Etakai read a part of the story was when Scilyn was meeting a girl in the palace. He had been sneaking around, but the girl found him and Scilyn was so alarmed he could hardly speak right.

"You were strange, Scilyn," Etakai muttered, shutting the book and returning it to the shelf. "But it seems your story is going to be just fine." Etakai gazed at the cover sadly. He had not expected himself to be jealous of the hero he had met inside the storybook. They had hated each other at once, but the facts remained that Scilyn was home while Etakai continued to wander in the Real World, looking for his story. He wished he at least knew what his book was called. He hadn't had a chance to look at it before it was taken from Shan's restaurant.

Etakai rubbed his eyes tiredly. It felt like years since he first appeared in the Real World and met Shan and Reitrin. The time spent in storybook worlds made it feel like an eternity.

"Hey, there," said a familiar voice.

A shiver went up Etakai's spine and he turned to find Fevros beside him.

The Eysheus' black hair was slicked back and he wore a fine suit with his fur coat hanging over his arm like a large dead animal. His lightning blue eyes held Etakai's gaze as if he was looking at a prize he wanted to win.

The look made Etakai uncomfortable.

"I heard your friend lost his restaurant," said Fevros, his wide smile crossing his face. "That's what happens when you let Garvon, Lord of Desolation, have free range anywhere. He's so disastrous things tend to go wrong around him. If only the Secret Police had not taken his story, you could have read it. It was quite good."

"What are you doing here?" Etakai asked with a glare. "And why are the clouds still in the sky if I gave you the blue jewel?"

The jewel was an item Fevros had had him hunt down in *The Lord of Desolation*. It was supposed to be magical and able to get rid of the black clouds, according to Fevros. Etakai did not trust the odd man.

"Sadly, that's not all I need to stop the clouds," said Fevros. "There is more I need, like your help."

"I am sure I can assist you," said Etakai. "What do you have for me to do?"

"Find a deserter," replied Fevros. He withdrew a book from under his coat and passed it to Etakai who took it and felt how heavy it was. "I want you to find the man and capture him. Once he is restrained, call my name, and I shall come and collect him from you."

"What is the man's name?" Etakai asked.

"Ace," replied Fevros. "You can take your friends into the story if you want, but know that you are the only one that can be around when you call me. If they are there when you call me, I won't come. Do you understand?"

"Sort of," replied Etakai. "How do I get inside?"

"I'm sure that girl you know will be able to get you in," replied Fevros.

"And how do we get out?" Etakai gave the man a dangerous look, which made Fevros chuckle.

"Oh, so stern. When you have the deserter I'll take you and the rest out. Just make sure you find him before time runs out."

"Time?"

"Yes, you have only a few hours to find Ace," explained Fevros. "Consider it a time trial. Find Ace before the time is up and you all get to go home."

"And if I don't find him?"

"If you don't find him, or you reveal your mission to any of your Real World friends, then I'll just leave you all in the story. It's going to be ruined after I take Ace out of it, so if I leave you then all of you will turn to ash with the book and be forgotten forever." He smiled wide at Etakai who was now pale.

"What do you mean?" He demanded.

"Books can die if an Eysheus removes a key component of the story," explained Fevros. "So, when Ace is removed, the book won't have long to live."

"You'd kill a whole world for one person?" Etakai demanded, waving the book in front of Fevros's face. "There are more people in here than your deserter."

"Well, yes, but they don't matter," said Fevros. "Hundreds of books are forgotten and lost forever. This one will join the ranks of those stories."

Etakai stood dumbfounded.

Fevros smiled at him once more before he turned and left the library.

Etakai looked at the book. It was called *The Dimension Jumpers* and had a colorful cover with spirals that glittered as if they were portals into different worlds.

"How can he act like a book dying isn't a big deal?" Etakai whispered.

Chapter Four
The Next Destination

Reitrin had to deal with Shan's long-winded list of changes they would make to the restaurant. He wanted the words "The Hideaway" to be shiny metal and hang above the door. Then he wanted to go through storybooks and make the food mentioned inside and also look up new kinds of tea that were in the books. Reitrin was getting a headache listening to him.

Shan was beginning to consider what furniture to buy when they arrived at the apartment. They took the elevator to Reitrin's floor, but when they arrived, Reitrin stopped outside the elevator with a shocked stare.

The front door was hanging open.

"Sia," Reitrin barked as she hurried into the apartment. "How many times has dad told you not to leave the–?" She cut off and stood petrified.

Shan hurried in behind her and also stopped.

Before them was a man familiar to Reitrin. His red hair was short and his eyes were black as night. He wore a white blouse with a black vest and black slacks. Despite how well he dressed, the sight of him made Reitrin's blood turn cold.

"Aoiro," she whispered. Her voice was thin with dread. "Why are you here?"

Aoiro, who was sitting on the arm of the couch with his arms crossed, frowned at her. "Well, I have a problem you see." His familiar voice making Reitrin tremble. This man had held her captive twice now and Reitrin was scared he would kidnap her again.

"What problem could you have?" Reitrin asked carefully.

"An old acquaintance of mine has taken an interest in that childish hero, Etakai," explained Aoiro. "I don't know what the man is up to, but he's given Etakai a book I would rather none of you enter."

"And why are you confronting us?" Reitrin asked. "We don't want to enter any storybooks. In fact we never wanted to." Behind her, Shan was looking pale and held his chest where the worse of his injuries was still healing.

"Indeed, I noticed this the last times we met," said Aoiro. "If you enter that story the consequences will be disastrous."

"They haven't already?" Reitrin recalled Etakai and Shan's injuries and her overwhelming fear that a storybook character would show up at any time to hurt them.

"It will be worse," replied Aoiro with an edge to his voice. His black eyes bored into Reitrin's and she felt a shiver go up her spine. "Etakai could very well become a danger to all of you if you enter the storybook he brings."

"But he's a hero," said Shan. His voice was small and Aoiro locked him in his direct stare, making the short man back away.

"He is no hero," Aoiro hissed. "I hope he learns this soon, for all your sake."

"Why do you care?" Reitrin demanded.

Aoiro looked at her glaring at him. "What do you

mean?"

"You're a villain," Reitrin replied. "You've kidnapped me twice and threatened Etakai also. You even told me you're a villain when you almost killed us in *Blood River*. Why shouldn't we defy you and enter the story? Is it your weakness? Will we be able to stop your evil schemes if we go in this book?"

"No." Aoiro was smiling at her, but the smile did not touch his dark eyes. "Clever aren't you?" He stood up and dusted off his pants. "I have given my warning, but now I must be off. I'm sure you both know why I cannot have Etakai find me here."

"Are you scared of him?" Reitrin asked coolly.

Aoiro straightened up and gave her a thin smile. "Why, Reitrin, why should I fear a man who does not even know who he is?"

Reitrin looked puzzled, but then Aoiro strode past them and left the apartment.

As soon as the door shut behind him, Reitrin glanced at Shan.

He was gawking at the closed door.

"Who was that?" Shan looked up at Reitrin who shook her head.

"His name is Aoiro," she muttered. "He's the one that removed Etakai from his story and left him in the Real World."

"So, does that mean he's Etakai's enemy?" Shan mused. "And, since we know Etakai, he doesn't like us and threatens us also."

"I knew all this was Etakai's fault," Reitrin grumbled as she opened the fridge and looked for something to eat. She didn't have time to search long before the door flew open again, nearly hitting Shan who shouted in surprise.

"What's the big idea?" Sia demanded, slamming the door shut behind her. "Of all the thoughtless things–"

"What are you going on about?" Reitrin lifted her head to glare over the fridge door at her sister.

"Ditching me at the diner," Sia cried.

"We had business to deal with," Reitrin retorted. "You knew we were leaving. Why are you acting up like this?"

"Because," Sia dropped into the couch with her arms tightly crossed. "My phone won't work and I got lonely."

Reitrin pouted. "Oh, I'm so sorry you felt lonely."

"You don't even understand," Sia scoffed.

Reitrin straightened at once. She slowly shut the fridge, though her fingers trembled. "Don't I?" Her voice shook with suppressed rage.

Sia did not catch the tone, but Shan did.

"Let's not start fighting, guys," said Shan with fear. He saw Reitrin's eyes were glazed from holding back her rage.

Sia had struck a nerve, and she had struck it hard.

"Fight?" Sia snorted. "I didn't say anything wrong."

"You're too daft to know when you say something wrong," Reitrin said with a cold glare. "Let alone when you say something right. You just let words fly from your mouth without a thought."

"Are you calling me stupid?" Sia jumped to her feet. "All I said was that you don't know what it's like to be lonely–"

"Don't I?!" Reitrin roared.

Sia gave a start.

"Who is left here alone every day while you parade around in the town over with all your rich friends?" Reitrin demanded. "Who is avoided because I'm blamed for our mother's death? And which one of us, Sia, is ignored by father like yesterday's news?" Reitrin was trembling with anger.

Sia crossed her arms. "So go make some friends."

Reitrin crossed the room in three strides and grabbed Sia by her collar and lifted her fist. Reitrin threw the punch, but someone caught her wrist first.

Startled, she rounded on the person.

Etakai looked down at her emotionlessly. "You may regret doing that. I don't blame you for wanting to punch her lights out, but it's not the best idea."

Reitrin scowled at him. She looked at Sia who stared at her in alarm.

"Fine," Reitrin muttered. She shoved Sia backward onto the couch and pulled her fist out of Etakai's grip. She went back to the kitchen and looked in the fridge again.

Etakai watched her then glanced at Sia who was glaring at the ground. She was shaking.

"I'm so glad you turned up when you did," Shan whispered to Etakai. "I didn't know what to do."

"It's not the first time I had to break them up like that," Etakai grumbled. He went to the kitchen where Reitrin was now going through the cupboards.

Etakai set the book on the counter in front of Reitrin.

She looked down at the book and her expression

sank to grief. "Who gave you that?"

"An Eysheus," replied Etakai. "He said we may find some answers in here."

"No." Reitrin left the kitchen.

Etakai grabbed the book and followed her. "I can't get in there alone," he told Reitrin as she headed to her room. Shan and Sia were watching them. "I tried but it's just a book in my hands."

"Then maybe you should play it safe and return it to the library."

"I can't. I need to find a way to get home and this book may have answers." Etakai didn't look angry. He looked a little desperate.

Reitrin watched him. "Something bad will happen in that book."

"How would you know?"

"Aoiro was just here."

Etakai stood motionless. His eyes scanned the room before landing on Reitrin again. "Why was he here?"

"He told us not to enter the book you brought here," she told him. "He told us you could become a danger to us all if we do."

"What nonsense." Etakai tossed the book to Shan who fumbled to catch it. "The Eysheus who gave it to me said there were answers in the book."

Reitrin watched Shan skimming the first page of the book.

"*The Dimension Jumpers*," he read, looking up at them. "How could this book answer any of our questions?"

"One of the characters in there knows what's going on," Etakai told him.

"What are you all going on about?" Sia was staring at them all with a bewildered frown.

"Oh," Reitrin went pale. She had forgotten Sia did not know a thing about book jumping.

"It's just a really good book," Shan said with a nervous laugh.

Sia snatched the book from him and flipped through the pages.

"We can't enter the book," Reitrin hissed to Etakai. "Not while Sia is here."

"I'm running out of time," Etakai snapped.

"What do you mean?"

"The person won't be there forever," Etakai replied. "We need to hurry up and find him or we'll miss our chance."

Reitrin saw the urgency in his eyes. Was it all a clever trap? Or would they be able to put an end to the Eysheus by finding the person Etakai spoke of?

"Okay," said Reitrin, heaving a sigh.

"Thank you." Etakai turned away from Reitrin to get the book, so he didn't see Reitrin's look of surprise.

She couldn't believe Etakai had just thanked her.

"What are you guys doing with the book?" Sia asked when Etakai took it from her.

"We're going to take it back to the library," said Reitrin. She motioned to Etakai and they left the apartment. The door shut behind them and Reitrin looked around.

"What are you doing?" Etakai asked, handing her the book.

"I didn't want Sia to see us vanish," Reitrin answered. "I guess here is good enough. We shouldn't be gone long enough for her to find the book lying here, right?"

"Hopefully," replied Etakai.

Reitrin took the book and watched as the sparkling lines on the book began to swirl and glow like a vortex.

"It's kind of scary," she told Etakai.

"Do I have to make you open it again?" He asked.

"No, I can do it," replied Reitrin. She looked up into Etakai's different colored eyes. "Hold onto my arm though. I don't want to be alone when we get there."

Etakai shrugged and took her arm.

Reitrin inhaled slowly before sliding her fingers into the pages and opened the book.

The white light burst from the pages and the black letters whirled around them as if they had been waiting expectantly.

Reitrin was surprised when she felt Etakai's grip tighten on her arm seconds before the ground vanished beneath them and the book snapped shut, lying in the middle of the empty hallway.

Chapter Five
Unfortunate Sia

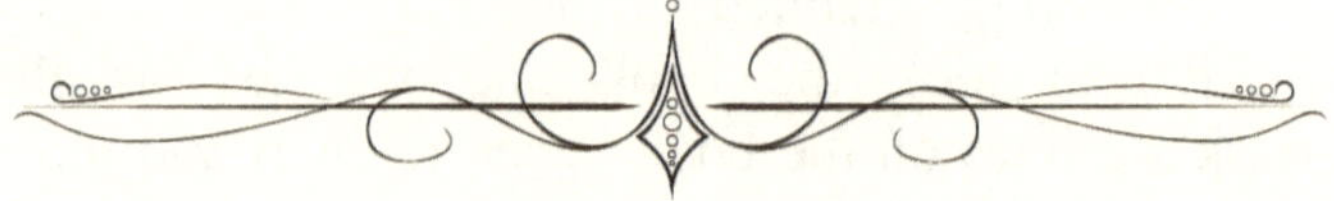

Sia was not sure what had just happened. One minute she was complaining to Shan about how rude Reitrin was, and the next she was sitting in a large field surrounded by woods and large boulders.

"Uh …" She stared at her surroundings. A bug landed on her hand but she was too dazed to shoo it away. The wind felt real. The smell of grass and dirt also appeared real.

She shook the bug from her hand and pinched her arm.

"Ow!" She jumped to her feet. She wasn't dreaming. The apartment had vanished and now she was lost.

Hopelessly and utterly lost.

"Reitrin?" Sia called, beginning to feel frantic. "Shan? Hello? Is anyone out there?" Her breath grew thin and it felt as if everything was closing in on her. She sank to her knees, holding her head and gasping for air. She was going to die out here. Where was she? What had happened?

Tears of terror rolled down her face and she rocked back and forth, unable to see anything but her panic in front of her eyes.

Something snapped and she jumped. She whipped around. Her gaze was unfocused as the stranger stopped his approach.

"Are you lost?" He asked with concern.

"Very!" Sia cried. She was shaking all over and

could hardly move. The tears weren't stopping and she was terrified the man was going to hurt her. This was it. He would kill her and she would never know what happened or why.

"It's okay, I'm a friend," said the man as he approached and knelt in front of her. He smelled like charcoal and grass. "Take deep, slow, breaths. Calm down." He set his hand on her shoulder and Sia felt her panic starting to ebb. She stared at the man's face. He had a kind face with dark stubble on his cheeks. There were spots of gray in his short black hair and his brown eyes were warm.

Sia relaxed a little, though she felt cold and clammy. "Who are you?" Her voice shook a little.

"I'm Alex," replied the man. He wore strange clothes. It looked like he was in costume pretending to be a ranger or something from a storybook. He wore a tunic, dark pants, belts laden with weapons and pouches, a sword, the dark cloak and tall boots. Sia was bewildered by the wear on all his clothes. It was like he was for real.

Like she was in a story.

"My name is Sia. Can you tell me … where I am?" She was even more confused when the question came from her lips. Her gaze traveled around the field again. The tall grass swayed in the breeze and saplings were growing here and there. It would have been a lovely scene if Sia at least knew how she had stumbled upon it.

"Oh, this land is hunting ground," explained Alex as he sat back on his heels and ran his hand through his hair. "No one has claimed it so it remains unnamed like most of the territory."

"I don't understand." Sia was shivering now. Though it was sunny, there was a chill in the air like autumn had begun. "Where is the city?"

"City?" Alex raised an eyebrow. "Are you unwell? There if no city except that of the kingdom, and I am sure you did not come from there. Your clothing is …" He stopped and examined her wardrobe. "Your clothing is odd."

"That's a laugh coming from you," grumbled Sia. "These jeans were fifty bucks, and this blouse cost me twice as much."

Alex straightened up and looked away. "I think it's happened again." He did not appear to be speaking to Sia.

Sia's stomach dropped. Was the man a lunatic? She inched away from him and stood up. "I should be going now. Please excuse me." She turned and walked away through the weeds.

"You'll only get more lost if you go that way," Alex called after her.

Sia waved to show she had heard and kept going. Her heart still raced from her panic attack, but she at least felt focused now. Her steps were confident, though she stumbled over rocks twice and had to stop to pick burrs off her blouse. She came close to the trees at the end of the woods, but as she came closer she stopped.

In the shadows were two glowing eyes watching her.

Shivers rolled up and down her spine and she wanted to step away, but her legs refused to move. The eyes were large, unlike any she had seen in the Real World. This was not a cat, deer, or raccoon watching her. Something different and frightening was before her. The creature shifted and Sia's heart leapt into her throat as it stepped from the shadows.

Its transparent paws were large as was its head. The shape was of a wolf, but its body was made of darkness that drifted from it like mist. It growled, the sound made the ground quiver.

Sia's knees gave in and she hit the ground. The wolf approached her, standing taller than any dog she had ever seen.

"Back!"

Sia jumped when a man with fiery red and orange hair shot past her and hurled a ball of flames at the wolf's face.

The wolf shook the flames off its face and snapped like a snake at the man who jerked back and hit the wolf with another ball of flame. It exploded on the wolf's face and the creature stumbled back, pawing at its eyes and growling. It turned tail and ran back into the woods, howling as it went.

"We're in trouble," said the man over his shoulder. "I think that one was a female and it may be calling for help."

"I didn't realize the shadow beasts had genders." It was Alex who spoke. He came up beside Sia and looked down at her. She was white as paper and stared after the wolf with terror.

"Flamelord," said Alex to the other man. "I think you and I have a more pressing matter than shadow beasts."

"Yes, I agree," said Flamelord. His charcoal black eyes looked down at Sia. "This girl is from the Real World."

Alex nodded. "Those damn Eysheus are at it again."

Chapter Six
Ace

Etakai sat up. He had landed flat on his back beside Reitrin who was staring at the sky. Their elbows were linked so Etakai slid out of her grip and stood up.

"There's a village nearby," he said as he peered through the sunlight towards the shine of distant roofs and rolling smoke from chimneys. "I think we should head there first."

Reitrin sat up and gazed around the rolling hills and tall weeds around them. There were farmlands far to their left with a large barn. She pointed to the barn. "I'd rather go that way."

"I'm trying to find someone," Etakai responded. "I need to ask people if they've seen him and find clues."

"Do you know anything about the person you're searching for?"

"Not really." Etakai shrugged.

Reitrin rolled her eyes. "What a great way to start your search." She pushed herself to her feet and dusted herself off. "I want to go look into that barn. Don't creepy people like hiding in barns?"

"What makes you think the person is creepy?" Etakai asked. "He may be pleasant."

"You really know nothing about him, do you?" Reitrin asked with annoyance. "You practically beg me to bring us into this book and you don't even know who you're searching for."

"I know his name," Etakai snapped.

"And what good is that if you won't tell me it?" Reitrin retorted. "I was hoping to help you with this so we could get home as soon as possible."

"I don't need your help," Etakai shot.

"Fine," Reitrin spun on her heel and strode away. "I'm going to do what I want. You can go get lost for all I care."

"Fine," Etakai yelled after her. "Don't get captured again. I won't save you."

"You didn't before," Reitrin shouted back. "So I don't expect you to."

With that they went their separate ways. Reitrin strode to the barn with her fists clenched and her mind spinning. She came to the corn field and walked along the edge until she found a grass path through the middle that led to the giant brown barn.

The ground was softer on the path and as she came to the other side she found the brown barn now appeared red.

"What the heck?" She muttered. She looked around and discovered there was a junk car, completely rusted, lying in the yard and a cart also. Horseshoes hung over the large doors and Reitrin approached slowly.

She stepped in a puddle and shook out her shoe. "The grass in the hills weren't wet," she muttered to herself. She looked around. Everything here was soaked.

Reitrin looked over her shoulder. The hills were still there and looked the same.

"Am I going crazy?" She wondered to herself. "It looks like it rained here, but those hills were dry."

"You're not crazy, no," said a grim voice from behind her.

Reitrin spun around to find a man standing by the barn. His skin was pale, his black hair chopped short and uneven. He wore an elegant suit with red ascot, ruby cuff links and sleek black shoes. In his hand he held a white mask that was cracked.

His black eyes looked hollow with misery.

"Who are you?" Reitrin asked.

"I'm ... I guess I'll let you call me Ace," murmured the man, leaning on the door of the barn. "Come in here, there's going to be more rain. It rains a lot in this dimension."

"Dimension?" Reitrin asked as she walked up to him. On closer inspection she found his clothes were not so fine. They were torn and filthy. "Were you in a fight?" Reitrin looked up at him with alarm.

Ace nodded, avoiding her gaze as he glanced back down the path she had followed. "And hiding in this dimension will only protect me for so long. Come in. I promise I mean you no harm."

A raindrop struck Reitrin's shoulder so she slid into the barn.

Inside it smelled of old straw, mold, and damp wood. Reitrin gazed up at the dark rafters. A lamp had been lit between a row of hay bales and it looked as if Ace had been making tea. A kettle hung over the lamp between a rude rigging of sticks and wire.

"What story are you from?" Ace asked as he let the door creak shut. "Or are you from the Real World?"

"The Real World," replied Reitrin cautiously. She wrapped her arms around herself and continued examining the barn. The rain was pattering outside and she shivered. "What about you?"

"Oh, I'm from this story," said Ace, picking up the kettle and peeking inside. He sighed and removed the lid.

Reitrin watched as he walked into the rain and set the kettle on the junk car where it would collect rain water. He then returned, shaking water from his hair.

"Sorry, I don't have enough water for two so I'm letting it fill more. It'll take longer to warm up though."

"I don't mind," said Reitrin.

Ace scratched at his head and uttered a curse. "I think staying in this barn gave me fleas."

"What happened to you?" Reitrin asked. "How do you know about the Real World?"

"I spent a lot of time there," explained Ace as he sat on the hay bale and gazed at the lamp. "I went back and forth, spying on one group and telling lies about the other."

"You were a double agent?" Reitrin moved to the hay bales and sat across from Ace. "Who employed you?"

"An Eysheus," replied Ace, looking at Reitrin. "I am sure they still know me by my fake name. I have stooped to giving out my real name for introductions just to keep myself safe. Ace; I hate my name." He shook his head and picked up his mask, gazing at the broken plaster sadly. "I suppose this was my fault."

"What is?" Reitrin asked.

"My current situation. Hiding in this dimension, waiting until it's safe to move. I asked for this when I accepted the job of a spy."

"Can you explain this dimension to me?" Reitrin asked. "How could I have walked right into a different dimension?"

"In the days of the original story you couldn't," explained Ace. "But then the Eysheus came. This story was full of dimensions to explore, and they wanted that ability. I don't know why, but one of them took the device of a dimension jumper and shattered it over a portal. When that happened some of the different worlds merged. I am hiding in this one because there is a protective barrier around it. It won't hold for long, but it will at least warn me if someone who means me harm comes in." He looked at Reitrin. "That's why I let you in. It's clear you're not here to hurt me, so I thank you. It was getting pretty lonely in this old barn."

Reitrin nodded and looked away. "Will you tell me the name of the Eysheus that employed you?"

"It's hard to tell who I truly worked for in the end," muttered Ace, spinning his mask as he spoke. "Fevros and Aoiro are both so powerful and have a great number of followers. I tried to be as clever as they, but then one of them sent their men after me. Being a dimension jumper I was able to transport myself back into my story, but now I'm in hiding because they will know this is where I've gone." He lowered his head. "I'm done for. When they find me they will kill me."

"Both?"

"Yes. Both of them have no mercy."

Reitrin shook her head. She did not understand. If both Eysheus meant harm to the world, why would they oppose each other? Was it some kind of competition?

"If you were a spy, then do you know what they were both up to?" She asked.

"I was only told what they could afford to tell me," muttered Ace. "So, in the end, they both discovered how useless I was. After that it all went downhill."

Reitrin gazed at him sadly. "I'm sorry." The rain outside grew heavier and Reitrin looked at the rafters. "When I approached this barn it was brown, but now it's red. Why is that?"

"Time changed as you passed through the portal," replied Ace, shrugging. "Passing through portals can cause all sorts of problems." He looked away and tossed his mask on the hay beside him. "I only hate that both Darklord and Flamelord were right about me."

"Who are they?" Reitrin asked.

"Dimension Jumpers like I was," grumbled Ace. "My superiors, much as I hate to admit it. They were granted powers by the dimensions and I was not, so I was always envious of them. They both hate me, but I'm sure they are my only hope of getting to a safe place where the Eysheus can't find and kill me. After all, if one of them kills me this book will turn to dust."

Reitrin rubbed her cold fingers together. "Maybe I can find them and tell them of the dilemma? My friend is supposedly a hero and I am sure if I tell him that saving you could ruin the plans of the Eysheus then he'd gladly help you."

"Really?" Ace looked more worried than hopeful. "Are you sure you can trust him?"

"I think so."

Ace heaved a sigh and placed his face in his hands. "Young lady, I tell you this as one who has experience. Don't trust people. In the end no one can be trusted. We all have a price. If someone finds that price then even your dearest friend would sell you."

Reitrin crossed her arms. "I don't believe that."

Ace looked at her, but then lowered his head and shrugged. "You'll learn the truth sooner or later. And then you would wish you had listened to me."

Reitrin shot to her feet. "I would never sell a friend. They're too few and far between."

"But would they sell you?" Ace glanced up at her. "It's likely your price is just higher than theirs. It exists, but I hope you never learn what it is. That would make you quite a trustworthy person."

"I'm done with you," said Reitrin. "But I still plan on helping you."

"Good luck." Ace stood up. "I'll walk you out. I need to retrieve my kettle. I also hope you didn't get any of the fleas in here."

They left the barn and once they were outside Ace turned to Reitrin. "I don't expect to see you again."

"You will," replied Reitrin. "And I'll have help with me too."

Ace shrugged. "I've given up. But still, good luck." He took the kettle off the car and returned to the barn.

Reitrin looked up at the raindrops falling on her head and ran her fingers through her hair. She was sure Etakai would help her, but Ace had managed to increase her doubt.

What would she do if Etakai refused?

"I'll do it myself," she answered. She strode down the grass path and as soon as she passed the corn field the rain cut off and the warm sun began to dry her damp clothes.

Chapter Seven
Flames and Darkness

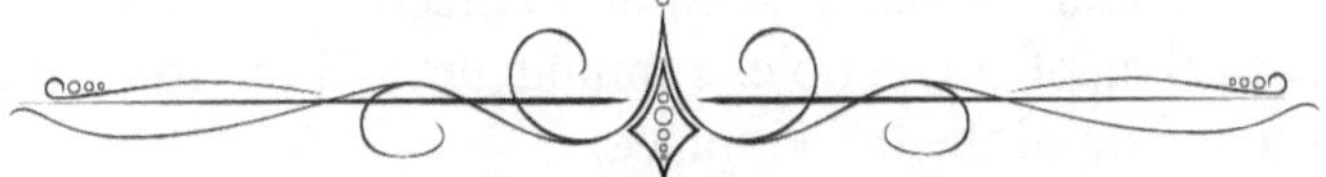

Etakai found no guards or soldiers in the large town. There were many shops and restaurants and a huge market square where traveling merchants set up shop for the day. It was loud and busy and Etakai sat near a meat merchant's stall to listen to passing conversation. He hoped to overhear something about dimension jumpers, Eysheus, or Ace. He stood beside the stall of a female jewel merchant. She was a loud woman telling her customers about a troop of soldiers she saw heading towards the town.

"They may pass by, but I don't know what they're coming here for," the merchant said to the customers that would listen.

"Scary." Some said.

"How weird." Others muttered.

Her exciting news was exciting only to her.

Etakai shook his head and moved on. Everything he overheard in the market was useless. There was no useful gossip, so Etakai switched to a more direct route.

He approached each stall and asked the dealer there if they had met a man named Ace.

Still no use.

Etakai was beginning to feel a little frantic. Time was running out and he still had no clue where Ace could be. Etakai kicked a lose stone against the side of a house and cursed. What was he supposed to do now?

"Etakai!" a familiar voice cried. A voice that sent a shiver of dread up Etakai's spine.

Etakai looked around and cursed again when he saw Sia, of all people, running up to him from the other side of the marketplace.

"You're here?" Etakai demanded.

"Yes," said Sia. Behind her was a man with an unpleasant look. He appeared to be guarding her and Etakai could not blame him for being uncomfortable.

"How long have you been here?" Etakai wondered. "You weren't supposed to come with us."

"I thought you two were just going to the library." Sia looked pale. "And I've only been here for a few hours."

Etakai scowled. "Reitrin went to look at a barn. You should go there too."

"I'm not there anymore," said Reitrin, making Sia jump a foot in the air. She had just come up behind them and frowned at her sister.

"You!" Etakai barked, making Reitrin give him a blank look. "How did you manage to bring her here?"

"If I understood how any of this worked then I'd make it all stop," Reitrin shot. Her anger melted at once as she spoke the next words, "I met someone who needs our help."

"Someone is in danger?" The man behind Sia was the one that spoke.

"Yes." Reitrin frowned at the man. "Who are you?"

"Alex," he replied, nodding to her. "I found this young lady in the hunting grounds and brought her here because she looked lost. Now that I see all of you I believe she is more lost than I first assumed."

"What do you mean by that?" Etakai arched an eyebrow at Alex.

Alex frowned at Etakai. "In a land of many worlds, people can become very lost."

Etakai did not like how much knowledge he saw in Alex's eyes. The man knew more than he was letting on and it put Etakai on edge.

"I met a man who is being chased by the Eysheus," Reitrin whispered to Etakai.

Etakai's eyes lit up. "What? You did?"

"Yes," said Reitrin. "I was hoping you could help me find the two people that he said could help him."

"Who are they?" Etakai withdrew a little at the proposal.

"I believe he called them Flamelord and Darklord," Reitrin replied.

"Flamelord?" Sia piped up and swung around to look at Alex. "Isn't that your friend?"

"Yes," said Alex, tilting his head and looking more unpleasant. "He would like to know who needs his help, especially if it may mean dealing with Darklord. They do not exactly see eye-to-eye."

"What's with the weird names?" Etakai grumbled.

"The man's name is Ace," Reitrin told Alex.

Etakai gave a start.

A burst of flame appeared before Alex and from it appeared a man with fiery orange and red hair.

Everyone except Alex stared at the man in surprise.

"Ace is in danger?" the stranger demanded.

"Don't make a scene, Flamelord," Alex hissed. It was too late though. Half of the marketplace had seen the fire and most were gawking at Flamelord and pointing at him.

"Where is Ace?" Etakai and Flamelord both demanded from Reitrin.

"The barn I went to," said Reitrin. "He's not–"

Alex cut into the conversation, grabbed Flamelord and Reitrin's wrists, and dragged them away from the crowd.

Sia and Etakai hurried after them.

"What's going on?" Sia hissed at Etakai. "That man came out of fire."

"You're inside a storybook," Etakai shot back at Sia. "This is the third time it's happened to Reitrin and I. We hoped if we left the apartment before we entered the book that neither you nor Shan would be caught up with us."

"What went wrong?"

"I don't know," Etakai answered.

"How did you get home before?" Sia asked. "Is there even a way? Are we trapped?"

"Of course there is a way," Etakai replied. "Stop asking questions."

Sia obeyed the order.

Alex led them down the curving streets of the town until they were surrounded by deserted houses.

"Now," said Alex, rounding on Reitrin and Flamelord. "I will excuse you all for that scene you made, seeing that this Ace guy means something to Flamelord, but I need to know who you people are." He eyed Reitrin and Etakai. Sia was standing behind them looking scared.

"We came here from the Real World," said Etakai.

"Etakai," Reitrin snapped.

"This story is used to different worlds," Etakai lashed back. "We may as well tell them."

"Don't argue," said Alex. "We know about the Real World."

"And we know about the Eysheus," Flamelord told them, crossing his arms. "In fact, Alex had a feud with one not too long ago."

"What?" Reitrin and Etakai were startled. Sia looked bewildered and pinched her arm again, wincing when it hurt.

"I must be dreaming," she muttered, slapping her cheeks.

"What was the Eysheus' name?" Etakai asked.

"Aoiro," grumbled Alex.

"Was he after Ace then?" Reitrin asked. "Ace wants you and someone called Darklord to help him find a place to hide where the Eysheus won't find him."

Etakai stiffened at her words.

Flamelord glanced at Etakai before turning to Reitrin. "Ace was always an arrogant showoff who wanted to be like Darklord and me. He was a traitor too, or so we learned from the Eysheus."

"What do you mean?"

"Skip the details," Alex muttered to Flamelord.

Flamelord sighed. "I'll help. We knew the Eysheus were using Ace. He was beginning to get scared near the end and he came to me for help, but I thought it was just another trick and didn't help him. I must ask you, was he wearing his mask when you spoke to him?"

"No," replied Reitrin. "He had it with him, but it

was broken."

"It's broken?" Flamelord frowned. He looked at Alex who was shaking his head.

"If we call Darklord we'll only accomplish drawing the Eysheus back into this story," Alex warned.

"And if Ace is killed for betraying the Eysheus then our entire story will dissolve," Flamelord replied. He had such a look of sincerity in his eyes it was hard for Reitrin to understand how Alex didn't melt right away.

"Do what you think is best," said Alex. He took one sweeping look of Reitrin and the others. "However," he muttered under his breath. "I've been tricked before by wanderers from other worlds. If any of you prove to be a threat, I'll cut you down without hesitance."

"Whatever works," said Reitrin. "Mister Flamelord, sir, can you contact the other man Ace mentioned?"

Flamelord gave a start, then laughed. "Just Flamelord, please. Alex is someone who should be called Mister Sir though." He cast a teasing look at Alex who glared back at him. "And yes, I can summon him."

Flames gathered in his hands. Sia and Reitrin watched in awe while Etakai studied his movements in silence,

Flamelord released a flaming hawk into the air. It circled above his head and then shot off into the air, vanishing in the sky as if it had been blown out.

"What went wrong?" Reitrin asked, searching for the bird.

"Nothing," replied Flamelord. "Darklord must be in another dimension."

"I'm confused," Sia muttered from behind them. "Can we go home?"

Reitrin rolled her eyes. "You aren't even supposed to be here," she shot over her shoulder at Sia. "We didn't want you here. Don't be a nuisance and stay close. These storybook worlds are dangerous." She glanced sadly at Etakai who still wore bandages.

"If Darklord comes quick we may be able to get you home," said Flamelord. "If you'd like, we could try. There's no guarantee you'd return to the world you came from. You just won't be here anymore."

Sia was shaking her head.

"Okay," said Alex. "What do we do now?" He looked at Flamelord who sighed.

"Don't make this more complicated for me, Alex," he muttered.

"Are you two using telepathy?" Etakai asked.

Flamelord and Alex gave him blank looks.

"Doing what?" Alex asked.

"Speaking to each other through your minds," Reitrin explained. "I was wondering it too, but I thought it would be rude to ask." She shot Etakai a glare.

"We have ways to communicate because of our bond," explained Flamelord. "You would have to read our story to understand. Darklord and Adrian had the same connection."

"Had?" Alex gave Flamelord a puzzled look.

"I never told you what happened to them," said Flamelord, hunching his shoulders. "The Eysheus interfered with their story."

"What!?"

Flamelord cringed at Alex's raised voice. "Darklord can still help us, but Adrian isn't really a part of the story line anymore."

"Won't that destroy the book in the Real World?"

"No, because Adrian is still in the story. We just aren't sure where he is."

Alex released a hard breath.

Etakai and Reitrin looked uncomfortable.

"Should we go?" Reitrin asked cautiously.

"We'll find you when Darklord arrives," said Flamelord, nodding once. "Find a girl called Leah. She lives with the blacksmith. If you mention my name she'll give you room and board as well as meals."

"Seriously?" Sia exclaimed. "Does such an angel exist in this world?"

"She isn't really an angel," said Flamelord with an awkward expression. "In fact the loss of Adrian out of the main story made her kind of ... brutal."

"That sounds better," said Etakai. He turned on his heel and left.

"Wait up!" Sia called, running after him.

Reitrin watched them go then turned back to Flamelord and Alex. "I hope Darklord won't take too long. I appreciate all your help. We're in this book because Etakai is looking for someone. You see, he's trying to get back to his own story." She explained Etakai's situation and Alex looked annoyed at the end.

"If he has been gone from his story that long, it is

possible the book no longer exists," he said. "But you and he still remember it?"

"Yes," replied Reitrin. "And, wouldn't he have vanished with the book?"

"We can't be sure," replied Flamelord. "The cause and effect of Eysheus are difficult to comprehend. They can destroy the book or keep it alive. It depends on what they're after and why they're even manipulating the storybook. There's no way to know for sure if they can destroy a book and keep a soul character alive at the same time or not without asking one in person."

"I see," muttered Reitrin.

"Will Darklord be able to get here when he receives your message?" Alex asked.

"Yes," replied Flamelord. "He should be here–" He cut off when a cloud of darkness wrapped around all three of them.

"About now," ended Flamelord grimly.

Reitrin was shivering as the darkness circled them. It hit the ground and evaporated, but standing before them was a man in a pitch-black cloak. The hood was over his head, but Reitrin saw his long black hair was oily and his skin was white as parchment. He looked at her over his shoulder and she saw he wore a scarf around his mouth and nose. His eyes were just as black as his hair.

"Darklord," said Flamelord with hesitance. "Did you understand the message I sent?"

Darklord rolled his eyes to heaven and faced Flamelord. "No, Sparky." His voice was as deep and cold as the shadows that had brought him to them. "I don't speak fire bird."

"This young lady claimed she has found Ace and he needs help." Flamelord motioned to Reitrin.

Darklord looked at her over his shoulder and his eyes narrowed. "She stinks of another realm."

"She's from the Real World."

Darklord's eyes widened and he whipped around to face Flamelord again. "Was it the same one that took Adrian? The Eysheus that brought her here, was it the same?"

"No, we can't be sure," Flamelord looked frightened under the weight of Darklord's glare. "She says they're after Ace though. She found him and he needs us to help him hide or they're going to kill him."

Darklord drew back and his ominous presence faded a little. He looked at Reitrin again, his eyes calmer than before.

"Describe Ace to me."

"Oh," Reitrin felt flustered. "Well, he's dressed in nice clothes, but they're kind of ruined. His eyes are black and so is his hair, which is short and chopped weird. He was also carrying around a mask that looked kind of important to him–"

"Master Death has fallen far," Darklord chuckled.

"He's still one of us," Flamelord interrupted. "Laughing at his downfall is pitiful."

"He would laugh at us if we fell," Darklord replied with a hint of acid. "So, young lady, where is Master Death hiding?"

"Do you mean Ace?" Reitrin trembled.

"Yes." Darklord scoffed. "The fool never received a name from the dimensions so he gave himself a name and paraded around like a child wearing a blanket for a cape. Who could blame me for laughing?" He shot a glare at Flamelord.

"It's pathetic, that's all," Flamelord growled.

"Are you two done?" Alex asked.

"We've only started," replied Darklord, looking at Alex. "I did not want to meet you again."

"Likewise," replied Alex grumpily.

"Where is Ace?" Darklord turned back to Reitrin. "If the Eysheus are after him we've little time to waste. We must go now."

"He's in an old barn," Reitrin replied, pointing in the direction of the field. "But it's some kind of misplaced dimension that the Eysheus caused."

"I've heard of stranger things," Darklord mumbled. He took Reitrin's arm and pulled her close. She felt the ground beneath her feet waver.

"Hold on," Darklord whispered in her ear.

Reitrin gasped. The world around her vanished in a swirl of darkness. When her feet touched the ground again she was dizzy and still clung to Darklord's cloak. She looked around, feeling puzzled by the rain. When she looked up she found herself in front of the barn.

"Ace!" Darklord shouted to the barn. "Your friend here consulted the wrong people. Get your things, we have to leave before they catch up."

Chapter Eight
Twisted

Ace raced out of the barn, panting and stuffing his mask in a tattered bag. He saw Reitrin and skid to a stop.

"I thought she was trustworthy."

"She is, but the ones she talked to aren't," Darklord replied. "We have to get you out of here before the Eysheus discovers your whereabouts."

"You knew where he was all along?" Reitrin breathed these words as Ace ran up to her and grabbed Darklord's free arm.

"He hid me here," Ace told her. "I have to maintain my image as the guy Darklord and Flamelord hate when I'm around strangers. I know I can trust Darklord. We work for the same–"

"Ace," Darklord growled. "Now isn't the time. Flamelord is coming."

Ace stared. "I didn't know Flamelord was a traitor–"

"Let's not start name calling." Flamelord appeared in a burst of fire. He stepped forward, a flame wrapping around his hand and arm. "Why so pale, Darklord?"

Reitrin felt Darklord back up, taking her and Ace with him.

"Flamelord, you're on the wrong side," Darklord warned. "I thought you were smarter than this."

"How on earth did you even find out?" Flamelord wondered, still moving towards them. "We were told no one would know."

"Why would you fall for that Eysheus and his lies?" Darklord barked. "If Ace is killed the book vanishes, and that means you and Alex with it."

"We were promised a new home," Flamelord replied simply. "Us and our few loved ones will be sent to the Real World where we can all live happily ever after."

"That's backwards," Reitrin said. She stared at Flamelord who watched her now. "It's storybooks that are supposed to have happy endings, not the Real World."

"Oh?" Flamelord was not convinced. "Well, I'd rather figure that out for myself, thank you." He lifted his hand and the next thing Reitrin knew she was hurled to the ground, but nothing stopped her fall. She kept falling, further and further into the darkness. Something snagged her ankle and she screamed.

As if tugged by a rope, the fall jerked to a stop and she fell on her back into the field of tall grass.

She sat up and looked around. She was outside the dimension of the red barn. Ahead of her was the village. She looked back at the barn, and to her alarm she found Ace was holding onto her ankle. That must have been what she felt during her fall.

Ace looked unconscious as he lay face-forward on the ground behind her.

Reitrin's head was spinning and she wondered if Darklord's ability to teleport was similar to how storybook jumping worked. Jumping into a storybook had never left her feeling dizzy though.

"Reitrin?"

Reitrin looked up and found Sia running up to

her. Behind her were Etakai and Alex.

Dread fell over Reitrin like a sheet.

A groan made her look over her shoulder. Ace was moving. He smacked his neck and started scratching.

"Stupid flea," he grumbled.

Reitrin looked wildly around, not knowing what to do. If Darklord said she couldn't trust anyone then that meant Alex was evil too, or was Darklord the evil one?

"Stay back!" Reitrin shouted as she stood up.

Ace released her ankle and pushed himself to his knees.

"Reitrin, what's going on?" Sia asked as she came up to her.

"Sia, get far away from here," Reitrin warned. She was eyeing Etakai and Alex. "I don't know what's going to happen, but it probably won't be pretty."

"What are you talking about?"

Reitrin stared past Sia to Alex and Etakai. Both had stopped when they heard her shout.

"Does she have a bump on her head anywhere?" Etakai called to Sia. "She's acting like more of a moron than usual."

"This story is twisted!" Reitrin called to Etakai. "Flamelord and Darklord are fighting to get Ace, and Alex is also trying to get him."

"Must be nice to be wanted," Sia muttered towards Ace. The man glowered at her.

"Reitrin, seriously," said Etakai as he shook his head. "What would anyone want with a mess like that?"

"Stay back," Reitrin warned again.

Alex stepped past Etakai. "Your friend is right," he told Reitrin. "We don't want Ace. I'm just trying to find out where Flamelord went."

Sia was the one that gave Alex a puzzled look. "Dude, use your weird telepathic thing then."

Alex stared at her. His face drained of color.

Etakai and Reitrin looked at him, but then Etakai slammed his knee into Alex's stomach.

"Get to the village," Etakai barked at Reitrin.

"No," Alex gasped. He grabbed his sword and drew it, lashing at Etakai who jolted back just in time.

"Come on," said Reitrin, taking Ace's arm.

"Darklord hasn't caught up yet, he must be having trouble," Ace said as he let Reitrin drag him through the weeds.

"Get back here," Alex roared as he turned to pursue them. He was tripped when Etakai swept his feet out from under him and then slammed his knee onto his back, pinning him to the ground.

"Go," Etakai yelled at Reitrin. "I'll deal with this one."

Reitrin nodded and ran to the village with Sia and Ace in tow.

"Get off," Alex cursed Etakai colorfully, but then Etakai drew a knife and held the point to Alex's nose.

"Now, listen carefully," Etakai purred in his icy voice. Alex froze. "I need Ace to get myself home, so you and your little fire-breathing pal won't interfere. Understand?"

Alex held his breath and looked up at Etakai whose green eye was glowing.

"What are you?" Alex whispered. His voice was

thin with fear.

"To be honest, I don't know anymore," Etakai replied. He knocked Alex out with one strike, then stood up and followed Reitrin.

Chapter Nine
The Dimension of Yull

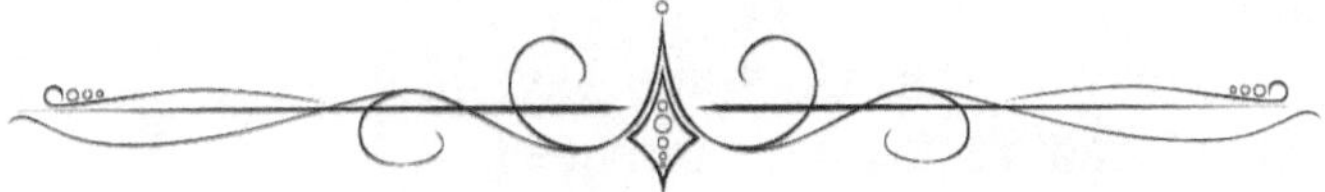

"Where can we hide?" Reitrin asked as she weaved through the houses, looking up and down the roads before moving on. Her side was beginning to hurt and Sia was panting for air behind her.

"The blacksmith … and the Leah girl … would give us food if we … mention Alex to her," Sia wheezed as she caught up to Reitrin and Ace and grabbed her sister's arm. "Reitrin." She crashed to her knees, still holding onto Reitrin's arm. "I want … I want to wake up now."

"You're not sleeping," Reitrin shot. "This is serious, Sia."

"Can't we go home?"

Reitrin cursed under her breath. "We don't have a way to get home."

Sia stared at her with terror. "What?"

"The dimension jumpers can't guarantee they would be able to get us home, and the Eysheus surely won't want us being able to meddle anymore. And–" Reitrin cut off, clapping her hand over her mouth.

Aoiro showing up in her apartment had put the warning from her mind completely. "The Secret Police will have us arrested for this!"

"Secret Police?" Sia looked dubious. "What are they?"

"A group of strange men that are trying to keep the Real World safe from storybook jumpers," Reitrin explained. She had no time to tell Sia everything though.

Ace tugged on Reitrin's sleeve and she looked at him.

He was staring at the sky, his face gray with sweat beading up on his forehead.

Reitrin followed his gaze.

Falling from the sky was what appeared to be a giant bubble. It fell fast, like a stone, and was heading for them.

Sia screamed, Ace whispered a prayer, and Reitrin held onto both of them. It was a dimension and they were about to find out exactly what dimension it was.

The bubble crashed, but nothing shook. It was like a feather falling on their heads, washing over their bodies like cold water, and then the world around them was different.

The village was gone. The houses were replaced by black ground and the sky was dark green and blue with dark clouds passing above, and two pale suns glowing faintly above them.

Ace dropped to his knees.

Reitrin was the only one standing. When she looked down at the others she found they were white as sheets and staring around with terror for different reasons.

"What just happened?" Sia cried.

"This … can't be happening," Ace whispered, his whole body trembling.

"Ace, where are we?" Reitrin asked.

Ace shook his head. He was trembling uncontrollably. "This is Yull." He pointed across the black ground. In the distance there rose a section of land suspended in mid air. There were roads wrapping around it like the rings of Saturn and the building that stood on it covered the whole plot of earth. It was like a majestic castle with fifty towers, each one a different shape and size, pointing to the sky.

"What's that?" Sia whispered. She looked around them. "Is this world dead?"

Ace swallowed hard and nodded. "I … I was the one that killed it."

Reitrin and Sia stared at him.

Ace covered his eyes with his free hand. "No. I don't want to be here. We have to get out somehow."

"I have no idea how far this dimension bubble spread when it landed," Reitrin muttered, looking around. The dead earth stretched for miles in every direction. The dimension bubble with the barn had been much smaller.

"There's always a way out," said Sia as she stood up. "I should know."

"How's that?" Reitrin gave her sister a blunt glare. "Weaseling out of paying for room and board won't help us here."

Sia scowled at her sister. "For your information, I first left you guys to go to college."

Reitrin blinked in surprise. "What? I had no idea of that."

"No, you didn't, because none of us talk." Sia kicked a stone hard and it flew across the dead ground, rolling in the dust and leaving a thin cloud behind. "You, dad and I never speak anymore. Ever since Mom died we never speak!"

"Sia, this isn't the time for a family therapy

session," Reitrin interjected. "We have to get home, and then we can talk about this. Please. You have to focus."

"How can I?" Sia sniffed and wiped the tears from her eyes. "How can I not want closure when we could die here?"

"We aren't going to die," Reitrin snapped. Sia was going to start acting dramatic if she didn't force her back into reality.

"Guys," said Ace, looking up at them. "We have company."

Reitrin and Sia looked around quickly. They didn't see anyone.

"Where?" Reitrin asked, grabbing Ace's shoulder and Sia's wrist. She was ready to run if she needed to, but something told her that running from anything in the dead world of Yull would be pointless.

Ace pointed to the sky.

They looked up.

A ball of fire was rocketing towards them.

"Just leave me to die," said Ace as he stood up. "It would be better that–"

"Shut up and run." Reitrin pulled both of them out of the way.

They ran across the dusty black ground and away from the fireball. It struck the earth behind them like a meteorite, leaving a long gorge and a smoldering pit. The fire made the rest of the world look dark and the trio stopped running to look back.

"It's Flamelord," Ace whispered to them.

Behind them, Flamelord walked out of the pit, dusting fire off his sleeves and hair.

"I guess we can't run?" Reitrin asked.

Ace was shaking his head.

"This place is crazy." Sia hissed to her sister. "Just look at all these handsome and powerful madmen chasing some beaten up guy in a nice suit. Your life is so exciting."

"Shut up, Sia," Reitrin grumbled. She was secretly impressed how handsome men could make Sia stop panicking.

"Give me Ace," Flamelord called as he approached them.

"No." Reitrin backed away, taking Ace and Sia with her. "What did you do to Darklord?"

"Restrained him," replied Flamelord. "Not that it is any matter to you." He kept coming. His footsteps left patches of fire. Embers from his entrance remained in his hair.

Ace knocked Reitrin's hand from his shoulder and stepped forward.

"What are you doing?" Reitrin hissed.

Ace placed himself between the women and Flamelord.

"If the book is fated to die this way, then I will allow it," Ace said, though his voice was weak.

"You don't want your book to die," Reitrin told him. "There has to be another way to stop this."

Flames shot across the ground, snapping at Reitrin's face. She stumbled back and held her cheek where a burn was forming.

"I was told you would have a quick death," said Flamelord as he stood facing Ace. He was taller and the soot on his face made him look like a demon. "But I hope you suffer for betraying the Eysheus for so long."

Ace held Flamelord's gaze. "You can kill me, here and now." He held out his arms. "I refuse to let the Eysheus do it."

Flamelord chuckled and lifted his hand. A sword of fire-red steel appeared in midair. He seized the hilt and drew it back then lunged at Ace.

His sword struck a shield of blue that shot Flamelord backwards, tumbling head-over-heels through the dust.

"I'd rather you not," said Etakai.

Reitrin and Sia whipped around. Etakai was striding up behind them, his blue eye glowing as he walked past them. As he passed the earth shook and the sisters looked around with fear.

"The book is running out of time," Etakai whispered to them as he passed. "My time to save this book is running out. I have to get us out of here right now."

"You?" Reitrin demanded. "How?"

"Start running," said Etakai, looking back at them. "The direction I came from. The dimension opens up into the original world of the story. You'll be safe there until my mission is accomplished and we'll all be sent home."

"Are you sure?" Reitrin asked.

"Yes, now go," Etakai barked. Flamelord had regained his feet and the ground around him was crackling with the fire of his rage.

Sia and Reitrin glanced at Ace, who met their gaze. "Go," he said. "You'll be safe if you leave me here."

"He's right," said Etakai to Reitrin. "Get your sister out of here. I'll protect Ace."

Reitrin hesitated, but then she and Sia ran away.

Ace scratched at his neck and looked up at Etakai who faced Flamelord. "You're a good liar."

Etakai glared at him. "Capturing you for Fevros will win me information on how to get home. And I want to get home more than anything."

Ace shook his head.

"Fevros?" Flamelord asked. "You work for him?"

"I don't work for him," replied Etakai. The ground rumbled around them again. In the distance Etakai saw the floating castle beginning to disintegrate like sand. "I'm out of time."

Flamelord turned to Etakai and hurled a spiral of fire at him.

Etakai's green eye flared to life, the green fire whirling down his arm. He knocked the fire away with the green flames and in the same motion threw three knifes at Flamelord with his other hand.

The knives slammed into Flamelord's shoulder, abdominal, and thigh.

Flamelord staggered back, his eyes wide and his body shaking.

"That knife in your gut will kill you slowly," Etakai said as he walked up to him, but then heard fast feet behind him.

He turned and a fist collided with his face.

Etakai's head whipped to the side. Blood and spit flew from his mouth. He staggered back, wiping his mouth and staring at Reitrin who was panting and shaking out her sore knuckles.

"Some hero," she yelled at him.

"What are you doing?" Etakai demanded. The

ground was trembling beneath their feet without stop and the disintegrating sand was coming closer. "The book is dying. You need to get out of here."

"No."

"Reitrin!" Ace cried and Reitrin looked to see Flamelord was on his feet. He lifted his sword with the last of his strength he hurled it at Ace.

Without thinking, Reitrin ran into its path. The sword caught her though the ribs.

Etakai's face drained of all color.

Ace stared.

Flamelord cursed and collapsed into the dust.

The world slowed to a crawl as the trembling earth caught Reitrin when she sank to her knees. The sword tip protruded from her back and glittered with her blood. She set her hand on the hilt and stared at the blood as it pooled over her fingers and gushed from her lips.

There was a flea on her hand, hopping up and down as if trying to get her attention.

Chapter Ten
Death of a Storybook

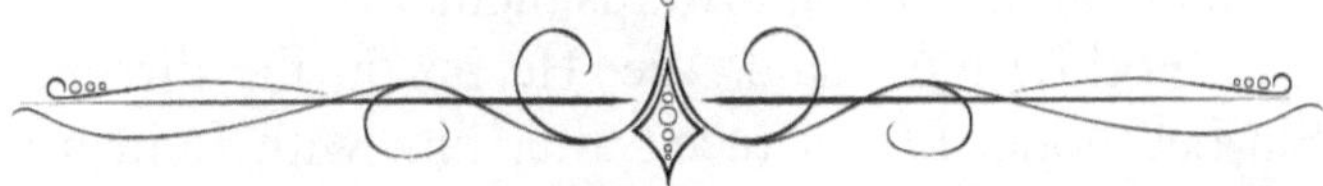

Etakai's mind jammed. He ran to Reitrin, holding his hand over the wound where the sword was buried. Flamelord was no longer a threat and the dying storybook's disintegration was coming closer.

"Reitrin …?" Etakai whispered, taking her shoulder. She was unconscious, but her eyes were still open and wide with panic.

"She must be dead," Ace said, crawling to them. "Why did she do that?"

"I … don't know." Etakai was bewildered and frightened. "Reitrin." He brought his arm around her shoulder. "Reitrin?" He felt her life was ebbing fast. "Wait." He was no longer thinking. His green eye glowed and he set his hand on her abdominal beneath the sword.

"Don't pull that out," Ace barked.

Etakai didn't listen. He pulled out the sword and Reitrin screamed. Her blood spilled out faster than before.

"Idiot," Ace yelled. "That will kill her faster."

Etakai ignored him as he dropped the sword. He set his hand over the wound and green energy slid down his arm and into her body. It wrapped around her and filled the wound. The blood that had begun to flow was stopped by the green energy.

"You're not allowed to die," Etakai told her. He picked her up and looked at Ace who was staring at him speechlessly.

"Get us out of here, dimension jumper."

Ace shivered and looked in the direction of the disintegration coming towards them.

"Follow me," said Ace. He ran in the direction Sia had gone. Etakai raced after him with Reitrin in his arms. Her breath was thin and her heartbeat fading.

As they went, Ace opened his bag and pulled out his mask. He slipped it on over his eyes and then whipped out an electronic device that had a glowing screen.

"Boss," Ace called into the device. "They failed to rescue the book. We need to evacuate now."

Reitrin's body heaved in Etakai's arms and she whimpered.

"Stay still," Etakai whispered. Ahead of them, the dead land was drawing to an end and they could see the village. Sia was standing on the other side, waiting and wondering where they were.

The disintegration sped up and it was nearly at their heels. Etakai and Ace ran harder, but Etakai's sight was starting to blur. He was using too much energy to keep Reitrin alive. The green flames were keeping her lungs breathing, her heart beating, and her mind thinking. Etakai was panting. He had never felt such weakness before.

Reitrin began to feel too heavy in his arms and his sight was going dark, but he forced himself to keep going. He had to get her out.

A buzzing sound came from the device in Ace's hand.

"We're out," Ace declared. He and Etakai passed through the dimension bubble into the sunshine.

"What happened?" Sia cried. The world was shaking around them and the sky was flickering from blue to gray. The people of the village were panicking and Ace looked around with a curse.

"It might be because Etakai killed Flamelord–" he began, but his words cut off when he saw Etakai.

The man was white as parchment and the fang tattoo beneath his green eye was growing down his face. Where it cut, black blood drizzled from his skin.

"What's happening to him?" Sia cried out in panic. "What's going on?"

Ace cursed and held his device over his head. "Get us out," he barked into the air. "Now!"

A burst of light and black letters wrapped around them. Ace smacked his neck again and scratched while cursing the flea.

Sia screamed as they all vanished from the world that crumbled into nothingness without them.

Five of them appeared in the hallway of the apartment.

Sia, pale, shaky, and panicking, looked around and found Shan was with them too. He looked just as scared as the others.

"We need an ambulance," Shan cried.

"How long have you been here?" Sia demanded, digging in her pockets for her cell phone.

"I'll explain later," Shan replied when Sia protruded her phone. Shan snatched it, dialed, and held it to his ear. "I was there the whole time."

Etakai was nearly unconscious. He could do little more than hold Reitrin close with the green energy beginning to weaken. It fizzled down to a thin stream and Reitrin turned white and went limp.

The book beside them crumbled to dust.

"No," Etakai whispered. His sight went dark.

He heard Sia and Shan calling to him and Reitrin, trying to get one of them to respond.

Etakai could not believe he had let this happen.

Chapter Eleven
Chaos in the Hospital

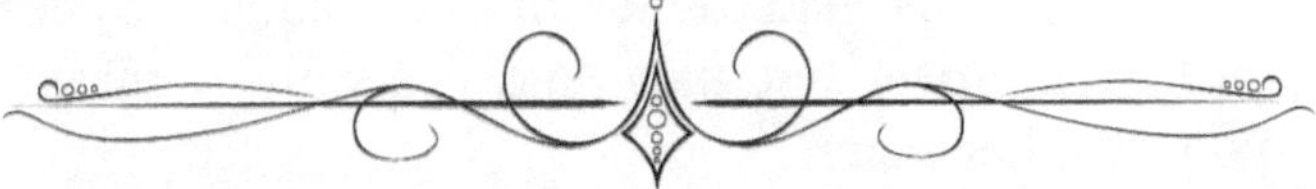

The hospital room was silent except the gentle beep of the heart monitor. No lights were on. Outside the black clouds grew denser and snowflakes fell to the streets despite being out of season. The city of Castroph was quiet.

Sia was sitting on a couch beneath the window. The small hospital room felt cold even though it was supposed to be a comfortable temperature. She watched her sister lying on the lonely bed.

Reitrin was wrapped in bandages, wearing a blue hospital gown with a bandage on her face, tubes in her body, and an oxygen mask over her face. Her skin was clammy and gray.

Sia drew her feet up onto the couch and hugged her knees.

The doctors said it was a miracle Reitrin was alive. The ambulance had arrived in record time. Shan had commented that it had to have already been on route to arrive as fast as it did. The paramedics worked fast and took Reitrin and Etakai out on stretchers.

Etakai was in a different room. Sia had only visited him while Reitrin was in surgery. Etakai had looked just as awful as Reitrin. The fang tattoo on his face had shrunk back to its normal size, leaving what appeared to be an ink stain on his cheek.

Shan, who had decided to stay with Etakai, said he had seen the tattoo lengthen before, but it had not drawn blood. Sia was too worried about her sister to care what Shan had to say concerning Etakai.

The doctors had done all they could to heal Reitrin's injuries, but they told Sia only a miracle could save her sister.

Now, as the snow fell outside and the machines forced Reitrin to keep living, Sia felt all hope was lost.

There came a soft knock on the door. It was the nurse. She did her normal routine, checking Reitrin's vital signs and asking Sia if she needed anything. Sia shook her head. She was too numb to know if she was really cold, hungry, or thirsty. The nurse left and the silence settled again.

"You know," said Sia gently, her soft voice sounding loud in the darkness. "I didn't hate you. I never hated you. I wish we had never stopped talking to each other. I just felt lost without Mom. Dad said you were to blame, so I blamed you." She hung her head and watched the tile floor. "I'm sorry. I can't really believe any of this. Who knew such things could happen?" She tried to laugh, but it sounded more like a sob.

Sia placed the back of her hand to her nose, but then looked outside at the snowfall. The flakes would tap the window and Sia hugged her legs tighter. The heater near her kicked on and the warmth momentarily wafted over her.

Another knock on the door made her look up.

It was Shan.

"Are there any changes?" He whispered as he shut the door behind him.

Sia shook her head. "How's Etakai?"

"He's recovering," replied Shan. "He woke up a moment ago and asked about Reitrin. I told him I'd check on her for him then he fell asleep again."

"There's no change," said Sia, gazing at her sister sadly. "You know, I had no idea my sister's life was so crazy."

"All this only started a few days ago," Shan explained as he sat on the couch beside her. He told her a little about the time in *Blood River* and how he had turned into a giant scorpion.

"How did that happen?" Sia asked blankly.

"I don't know," replied Shan with a shrug. "But being a flea this time was no less unpleasant."

Sia gave a start. "You were a flea?"

"I clung to Ace for dear life the whole time I was in that book," Shan replied, rubbing his neck. "Thank goodness a flea is so durable. That man hit me so often it was almost impossible to see what was going on."

"What was it like?"

"I really hate dandruff." Shan smiled sadly and shook his head. "I forgot I was human from time to time, but whenever Reitrin or Etakai were around I regained my senses and could understand what was happening. I had never seen anything as horrifying as Reitrin running in front of Ace and taking that sword for him."

Sia bowed her head. "So that's what happened. My sister sacrificed herself for Ace. I don't understand her at all."

"I think she had to step up and be the hero," Shan muttered. "Etakai was not acting like himself. I mean, he was, but it almost looked like he was after Ace also. The way he acted when Reitrin and you left him in Yull was frightening."

Sia rubbed her arms. "I think I'm hungry now."

"We can get something to eat from the vending machines downstairs," Shan said as he stood up. "They probably closed the kitchen for the night."

Sia stood up. She took a long look at her sister before leaving the room with Shan.

The door shut and silence filled the room again. It was broken by a long sigh.

"About time," muttered Ace as he stepped out of the shadows. His clothes were no longer ruined and he wore a fedora with a red feather. His mask was repaired and he approached Reitrin's bed.

He tilted his head as he watched her. "No one has ever bothered to die for me. So, because of that, I went to extra lengths for you." He removed a small bundle from his pocket and opened it. Inside the rag were pale purple leaves that sparkled.

"I was keeping these for myself," he said to Reitrin. "They won't heal you completely, but if your will to live prove to be strong enough then you will survive because of them." He set the leaves over the bandages of her abdominal and they melted like ice, seeping into the bandages and leaving a glittery residue on the cloth.

Ace drew back and watched the heart monitor.

Nothing changed.

Ace sighed. "I thought you were stronger than that."

"Don't insult her."

Ace looked over his shoulder. He had not realized Aoiro was with him. The redhead was sitting on the couch with his arms crossed and a look of contempt on his face.

"Aoiro," said Ace, nodding to him. "Are you going to kill me?"

"No."

"Gods, what a relief." Ace sighed. "I thought you wanted me dead for real when you didn't evacuate us right away."

"I was busy." Aoiro stood up and moved forward to look down at Reitrin. "I received the information I needed, but I wish we could have saved your story. I didn't think Fevros had so many men on his side."

"So, Fevros was serious."

"Yes." Aoiro narrowed his eyes. "I never expected anything less from him." He faced Ace again. "Do I have your loyalty now?"

"As much as I have," Ace replied. "Loyalty isn't exactly in my nature."

Aoiro frowned, but then looked outside. "They're here. Make yourself scarce."

Ace bowed and then disappeared into the shadows.

When he was gone, Aoiro looked down at Reitrin. "If you lost your will to live after saving another life then you are no hero. Keep living. I still have use for you." He then disappeared right before the door flew open.

"Hang on," The nurse protested as the man in black clothing turned on the lights. "You can't take a patient without proper papers."

"We aren't here to take this one," the Chief shot at the woman. He wore sunglasses and his black hair had strands of silver. "I just wanted to see her condition for myself." He stood over Reitrin and stared down at the bandages. The glittering residue lingered and he shook his head.

"Master Death was here."

The nurse looked scared and jumped when Shan and Sia raced into the room.

"What are you doing?" Sia demanded. She held a bag of chips and a soda in her hands.

"Checking on the fugitives," Chief replied.

"They aren't fugitives," Sia argued. "And who are you anyway?"

Chief pushed past them without an answer and left the room.

Sia cursed after him.

Shan followed Chief as he went to Etakai's room and threw open the door. Inside the bed was empty, the window was open, and all of Etakai's things were gone.

Shan stood dumbfounded.

Chief searched the room. "He must have known we were coming." He whipped out his phone, dialed, and placed the phone to his ear as he left. Shan heard him ordering his men to find Etakai.

Shan stood in the empty room, staring at the curtains flapping in the wind. Etakai must have pretended to be asleep. He had given Shan a reason to leave so he could make his escape.

Etakai had played him.

"Some hero," Shan said, clenching his fists. "His story was so wrong about him. That guy is the furthest thing from a hero."

Chapter Twelve
On the Run

Etakai's head hurt as he ran down the snow-covered street. The sight of his green eye was blurry from all the energy he had used. He rubbed it frequently.

The sirens of the police cars searching for him echoed up and down the city. Etakai knew they were after him. He had been hiding under the window when the Chief and Shan entered his hospital room. Shan's words had cut Etakai deep.

"That guy is the furthest thing from a hero."

Etakai winced and ducked into an alley. He leaned against the cold brick wall, panting and wiping sweat from his brow. Shan wasn't wrong. Etakai didn't know what was wrong with him. He was acting more like a villain. He had tried to get home, but every attempt put innocent people like Shan and Reitrin in danger. Now, as he stood hiding in the darkness, Reitrin's life was in limbo and he was as much to blame as the sword that pierced her.

Reitrin should have never had to interfere.

Etakai looked up when he saw flashing lights approaching. He ran down the alley, turning down the next street and hurrying down the road.

From the darkness a gun fired and Etakai crashed to the ground to avoid the shot. He rolled over and looked up as a man dressed like the Chief, but with blonde hair, stepped out of the shadows.

"Found you," said the man, pointing the pistol at

Etakai's chest. "Now, come with me quietly and you won't get hurt."

Etakai's blue eye blazed and a shield came up between them. The man fired, but the bullet hit the shield and fell to the ground. Etakai jumped up and ran away.

"Get back here!" The man roared. He shouted into a phone he carried and the next thing Etakai knew he was being followed by two more men in black.

Etakai dived into the nearest alley and leapt straight into the air, catching the nearest fire escape and climbing it to the roof. As soon as he was at the top the two men chasing him landed on the roof in front of him.

"You're not the only storybook character out here, Etakai," said a man with a voice as sly as a snake. He and the other wore the same body armor and helmet as the last officer, but he carried two swords and the man beside him with short white hair had no visible weaponry.

"Why are you after me?" Etakai asked, searching for the best chance of escape.

"You're a threat," replied the man with white hair. His voice sounded kind, but there was gravity to it that told Etakai there was no mercy in him. "We must take you into custody before you cause more trouble."

Etakai shook his head. He hurled a knife at each man and they deflected them with ease, but Etakai had no intention of fighting. He leapt off the roof, landing on the one behind him, and took off across the rooftops. The officers pursued him, alerting their

Chief that he was on the move.

Etakai was frightened. He jumped across wide spaces, hoping the officers would lose him, but each time he glanced back they were close behind.

The line of the city shrank and Etakai leapt off the last tall building, speeding towards a small house. He landed, rolled, and when he popped up a burst of light met him. He shouted, but had no chance to stop himself for falling into the light.

He crashed to the ground and the portal snapped shut above him.

Etakai jumped up, looking around frantically.

He stopped.

The portal had taken him to the library.

Bored applause made Etakai turn to behold Fevros sitting on one of the reading tables. He wore his fur coat and his blue eyes were lit with amusement.

"It will be a few minutes before they can trace you here," said Fevros as he stood up and approached Etakai. "I must admit, your performance in the last book was disappointing. I hoped you would let the girl die and call me. That would have accomplished your mission perfectly, since the girl would never have witnessed it."

Etakai recoiled. "You … you really don't care who dies, do you? Even people from the Real World. Just what are you?"

"Oh, I'm only an Eysheus," said Fevros with a laugh. "We're a little twisted."

"We?" Etakai asked, watching as Fevros went to the shelves labeled History and began to search them.

"Yes," replied Fevros. "Aoiro and I are the only

real Eysheus in existence."

"I don't understand," said Etakai, placing his hand over his head.

"Oh, does your head still hurt?" Fevros asked, glancing at him from the corner of his eye. "Using as much energy as you did I'm not surprised. You did recover quickly. I'm impressed."

Etakai shook his head. "I'm starting to think impressing you is the last thing I want."

Fevros laughed out loud and removed a book from the shelf. "Yes, you're right. Now how about we fix the problem?"

"Problem?" Etakai asked.

"Yes," said Fevros, stroking the book as he smiled at Etakai. "I can see you're confused. I don't blame you. It's hard to tell friend from foe in our little game of book jumping."

Etakai wrinkled his brow. He wished he was not so groggy. There had been no time to completely recover from trying to save Reitrin. He was weary and Fevros's confusing talk was not making matters better.

"Just what are you after?" Etakai asked.

Fevros shrugged. "You'll find out soon enough. The Secret Police are almost here. Will you accept one last test?"

"Are more people going to die?" Etakai growled.

Fevros chuckled. "Well, you're going to a place where a lot of death happens every day. And you're going because I want you to."

"And if I refuse?"

"Can you?" Fevros smirked at him. "You fell into the portal and I brought you here. What makes you think you have any chance of escaping me?"

Etakai scowled.

"And do you really think you have a chance of surviving this Real World?" Fevros added. "After all, once Reitrin is dead you'll be shunned from those people who may have accepted you."

"They never would have," Etakai retorted. He looked away, trying to ignore the guilt that filled him.

"Are you so sure?" Fevros inquired. "After all, you were the one pushing them away. They were okay with you, even though you were a fictional character. I almost venture a belief that you were starting to enjoy being around them."

"No way," Etakai barked. He winced and held his head. "There's no way."

Fevros lifted his hand and pointed at the ceiling. "Do you feel that?"

Etakai lifted his head and tried to sense what Fevros mentioned.

"Can you hear it?" Fevros asked. "That girl's heartbeat. It's so faint, despite your desperate attempt to save her." He grinned at Etakai. "And you know what? She'll die if you enter another book."

"What?" Etakai demanded. "You're lying."

"Her life is tied to your presence due to you using your green energy." Fevros snapped his fingers. The words in the book swirled and Fevros turned it to face Etakai who stepped back. "You should have just done what I wanted," Fevros told him as the light wrapped around Etakai. "Now go away and think about what you've done."

"No, wait," Etakai shouted.

The light erupted around him and he was sent

into the book. He heard Fevros laughing and Etakai yelled for help.

"Decide to be my loyal servant and I'll save you," he heard Fevros tell him. "Defy me and you'll die in this book."

The light vanished and Etakai was gone.

Fevros shut the book and returned it to the shelf. "You're such a fool outside your story. That's too bad. You could have been a great help." He looked up when he heard the doors of the library open.

The Secret Police raced into the library and Fevros was faced by three men.

"Where's the fugitive?" The man with blond hair demanded.

Fevros grinned and waved at them. In a burst of light he disappeared and the officers stood in dumbfounded silence.

"Dammit, that was Fevros." the blond told the others. "I've never seen him in person before."

"If he has Etakai then we're in trouble," the man with white hair whispered. "We need to secure the others just in case Fevros is going after them next."

"Alert the Chief," said the blond, turning and leading them out of the library. "Have him station more guards outside the hospital. We're in trouble."

Chapter Thirteen
Darkness of the Mind

It was like a black and white movie playing out before Reitrin's eyes. She could not distinguish who was who or where they were, but she heard their voices and saw their movements. Everything Shan and Sia said about her and Etakai. Shan was the flea? He sure gave Ace a hard time.

Ace. Reitrin heard him too. He was telling her he was sorry. Something touched her paralyzed body and color began to fill her dream. She heard shouting and a confused atmosphere filled her head. Chief, the leader of the Secret Police came in. He did not linger and he appeared to be frightened and angry.

Why was Reitrin hoping he was okay?

They left and Sia lingered. She was pacing and waiting. When Shan returned he told Sia that Etakai was missing. Sia was startled. Reitrin was not. She knew Etakai would never linger when he sensed danger. The man claimed to be a hero, but he didn't act like one.

Reitrin thought she could hear him. Perhaps his green energy that had kept her alive made her aware of him? She felt his panic. He was filled with fear and in pain. Etakai was running away and being chased. His heart jumped when there was gun fire and he had to flee again, using blue energy to make a shield.

There was more. Etakai was frightened and tried desperately to escape. He ran, he fell, and was transported to the library. A chill went through

Reitrin. He was with a stranger. A powerful and frightening stranger. Reitrin was scared. She wanted to call to Etakai and tell him to get away. They were in the library for a while but then Etakai's presence vanished.

He was gone.

"No!" Reitrin shot out of bed, but then fell back into the covers with a scream of pain.

The heart monitor was beeping rapidly and Reitrin struggled to move, but she was covered in wires with a mask on her face. She was frightened and two nurses came into the room to calm her and make sure she had not caused any damaged.

"Reitrin?" Shan and Sia called.

"Out!" The nurses ordered. The doctor raced in and Reitrin saw Shan and Sia being forced out of the room.

A mask was pressed to Reitrin's mouth and nose and she breathed in the gas, feeling herself fall asleep. She was still aware. They were checking her wound, talking about how strange it looked, and shocks of pain went through her body. Reitrin gripped the sheets and when her eyes opened again the room was light and the curtains were open, showing the dark clouds and snow collected outside.

Reitrin set her hand over her abdominal and carefully sat up. She winced, but the pain was not as intense as before.

She realized she was not alone and looked at the couch to meet the gaze of Aoiro. He watched her with one arm stretched out on the back of the couch and a book in his other hand

"About time," he said. "You're quite a

troublesome girl, did you know that?"

Reitrin examined him. He wore casual dressy clothing, a black blouse and matching slacks. His red hair was brushed and looked soft.

"You're not panicking," said Aoiro.

Reitrin shook her head and sat back, leaning against the pillows and setting her hand over her abdominal. "Where are Shan and Sia?" It hurt to speak.

"The kitchen is open," replied Aoiro, setting the book aside. "They're getting breakfast."

"So they know you're here?"

"No, of course not."

Reitrin frowned at Aoiro. "Are you going to kidnap me again?"

Aoiro laughed and shook his head. "No, you're in no condition for that kind of excitement."

"So, what are you doing here?" Reitrin asked.

"You sacrificed yourself to save Ace," replied Aoiro. He stood up and approached her. "Well, you did that after punching Etakai in the face. Needless to say, you're more than an average girl, Reitrin."

Reitrin pouted when he used her name. "If Etakai wasn't going to act like a hero then I had to."

"And I need you to be the hero again," Aoiro told her.

"What do you mean?"

Aoiro sighed and sat on the edge of her bed. Reitrin was not okay with this. Aoiro didn't care.

"Etakai was sent into a historical fiction," he said. "I'm familiar with it. It's a poorly written rendition of the civil war which happened on this land before Castroph City was ever built. It's a story where women can be captains and prisoners are treated badly. It's not a great book historically-speaking, but the danger inside will be real, and someone like Etakai won't know how to survive. He's in terrible danger."

Reitrin rolled her eyes. "And you care why?"

"If he is left in that world too long he could be lost forever." Aoiro looked at her. "My enemy, Fevros, sent him there. If Etakai is left in that world with no hope of rescue he could quickly turn to Fevros for help. If that happens he will be a stronger enemy than anyone I've ever faced."

"Is that a long list?"

"Sadly, yes." Aoiro shrugged. "However, were you to go in after Etakai, I'm sure you would be able to knock some sense into him."

"And why would I do that?" Reitrin asked.

"Oh, I don't know," replied Aoiro. "You seem to be a clever girl. Come up with a reason."

"I have a reason," she replied. "I'll go because he needs a good kick in the head."

Aoiro grinned at her. "It's not going to be easy."

"I am aware of that," muttered Reitrin. "I studied history. Even if it's badly written and historically inaccurate, it's going to be ugly. What time am I going back to?"

Aoiro picked up the book off the couch and handed it to her. "I think it's a couple hundred years back," he told her as she looked at the old cover. "When war plagued this land. This is the only history book in the city that records a time when the sky turned black with clouds."

Reitrin gave a start and stared at Aoiro who

nodded once. "I was just reading it," he told her. "I think these black clouds may have an explanation inside this book. You may be able to accomplish more than you think if you go in."

Reitrin hesitated. "Why don't you go? And why would you want me to? I thought you were a villain?"

"Are not all of us a villain to someone?" Aoiro grinned and Reitrin felt as if she had seen the kind look before.

"You're up to something," she told him.

"Always," replied Aoiro. He handed Reitrin a belt. It was wide and made of thick leather and on the inside there was some kind of soft fabric that almost looked like a species of plant.

"This belt will keep your wound from bothering you," he told her. "Wear it always. Keep it dry. Do not remove it unless I am there. Do you understand?"

"I guess," said Reitrin, frowning. "But why would you help me?"

"I have my reasons," replied Aoiro. "And they're good reasons. I can't enter that book because Fevros has blocked me from it. However, you can get in."

"I thought you were the one bringing us in and out of books," Reitrin said with a puzzled look. "I'm not magical. How could I get in without help?"

Aoiro shrugged. "You've done it before. I had no idea where you were until you stumbled into *Blood River* by yourself. I had no part in that. Neither did Fevros."

Reitrin gawked at him. "How will I get out?"

"You'll figure it out," Aoiro replied. "Here are your clothes. You can't go running around history in a hospital gown." He placed a bundle of clothes on the bed.

Reitrin slid them towards her and hid them under her blanket. She then looked at Aoiro. "Why were you looking for me? You mentioned before that you had been searching for me."

Aoiro heaved a sigh and shrugged. "Because I lost you a long time ago." He looked down at her and for a moment just held her gaze with a calm smile.

"Be safe." He nodded once and then vanished in a burst of light and letters.

Reitrin jumped when the door to her room opened.

Shan and Sia walked in with food trays.

"You're awake!" Sia exclaimed. She set her tray on the bedside table and took Reitrin's head in her hands, kissing the top of her head and laughing.

"Sia," Reitrin stammered, embarrassed by her sister's rare and unexpected affection. "What's gotten into you?"

"I was so scared," Sia cried. All of a sudden she burst into tears.

"Good gosh, calm down," said Shan as he set aside his tray and pulled Sia away from Reitrin. He helped her to the couch and patted her arm.

"What's happened since we returned?" Reitrin asked.

Shan filled her in on all that had happened. None of it surprised Reitrin. She truly had witnessed everything.

At the end of their story, Reitrin looked at the book on her lap. She stroked the cover and frowned.

"Etakai is in danger," she told them.

"With the Secret Police after him, I'm sure he

is," Shan muttered, sipping the orange juice he had brought with his food.

"No, I mean serious danger," said Reitrin, looking at them. "He's stuck inside a historical story and I'm going to find him."

Shan and Sia gawked at her.

"You're in no condition to go book jumping," Shan hissed just in case people were within hearing distance.

"Etakai saved my life," Reitrin retorted. "As foolish as he may be, I have to return the favor."

"You can't," Sia begged. "I have so much I have to talk to you about. With father missing we may be the only family we have left and I don't want us to hate each other."

Reitrin stared at Sia, but then shook her head. "I'm sure I'll be back. Just keep this book in a safe place for when I return. Make sure there's room enough for both me and Etakai."

Sia and Shan were startled when Reitrin opened the book then and there. She set her hand on the pages as the words began to swirl and the light and black letters filled the room, circling Reitrin and then they and Reitrin vanished and the book fell shut on the empty bed.

Sia shot to her feet. "What has she done?"

Shan shook his head. "We need to get that book to a safe place."

Chapter Fourteen
History

BANG!

Etakai's eyes flew opened. He gasped, looking around as the explosion went off. Smoke and dust went flying. Etakai ducked behind the piles of sand bags, holding his helmet as another bomb blew up only feet away from where he hid.

"When did the enemy find us?" he cried to his companion. "I wasn't asleep for that long. I thought they'd be attacking at dawn."

"They snuck up on us," a man named Charles shouted. He leaned back against the sand bags that formed a wall of protection. Above them there was a fence of barbed wire stained with blood.

"We didn't know they were coming until it was too late!" Charles called. "Dirty bastards."

Etakai rolled his eyes. He crawled to the top of the pit, looking over the edge at the long hilly ground covered in fences of barbed wire, pikes of sharp wood, dead bodies, and black trenches where bombs had gone off. There were mud puddles and dead trees everywhere. Etakai slid back down feeling sick.

"Have a nice dream?" Charles asked jokingly. His face was smudged with dirt and grime. None of them had had a chance to wash for months.

"Not really," Etakai called back over another explosion that was a little farther off. They heard a chorus of men cry out in pain, followed by screams and another explosion, but there was no gunfire.

"Too bad," Charles shouted with a light smile. "Dreams are a nice break away if one can settle their mind enough to conjure a good one."

Etakai forced a grin as he readjusted his helmet. Charles was the only ray of light in the turmoil. Etakai couldn't help but be drawn to the bright attitude of the lieutenant. The man was cheerful about everything, unless they were charging headlong into the battlefield.

Charles was the one that taught Etakai how to use firearms.

The first charge Etakai had experienced had been hell. He hadn't known what was going on and would have died if Charles hadn't dragged him out of harms way. Etakai had tried to fight him off, having been unsure as to who was friend and foe, though at that point in time he had seen everyone as an enemy. Charles had brought him safely through the attack, showing him a place he could hide while waiting for the noise to die down. Etakai had sat alone, clinging to the strange weapon he didn't understand.

Someone had run by him, but tripped and fell into the barbed wire. His strangled cry of pain still haunted Etakai's mind.

"How could someone hope to conjure a good dream in this world?" Etakai wondered when the explosions around them died down. Charles peeked over the barricade, shifting his gun to his shoulder before kneeling beside Etakai.

"I can sometimes," he asked lightly. "But they always end a little too soon."

Etakai flinched when another explosion went off and Charles slid his gun back into his grip and crawled to the top of the barricade, looking around.

"The tanks are heading away from us," he murmured, sinking back to the ground. "We managed to escape with our lives for now."

Etakai glanced at Charles, but then leaned back against the sandbags with a sigh. He held the gun in his hands, having learned to never put it down when in the midst of a battle.

In this story the war was life. Etakai had fallen into the middle of it and instead of being killed he was rescued, but then recruited against his will. Not a word had been said about his eyes or his tattoo, and no one had questioned his lack of a last name. They had given him a dark green uniform, a helmet, a gun, and instructions on how to use it, and the next thing he knew he was shoved in a pit with a group of men he didn't know fighting a war for reasons he didn't understand.

"How long has it been since I joined?" asked Etakai, his eyes closed. Sleep threatened to come over him again, but it was delayed when Charles fell to the ground beside him and popped open a water flask.

"You?" He inquired, rubbing his chin before taking a swig of water. He sloshed it around in his mouth before swallowing. "I'd say two months." He nodded and passed the flask to Etakai who opened his eyes to examine it before accepting and taking a drink. The water tasted like plastic. His throat was parched and he coughed when the water tickled his throat.

He handed the flask back to Charles and then lay back, gazing at the cloudy sky above him. It might not have been clouds, but the smoke was so thick he couldn't tell it apart. More explosions rumbled through the ground and Etakai looked at Charles.

"Any word of where we're heading next?"

"There's been no word from HQ.," said Charles.

Etakai saw a frown on Charles's face. He slipped off his helmet, his blonde hair wavy and held back in a ponytail with a rubber band. Charles rubbed his sweaty head before putting the helmet back on.

"In fact," he murmured, letting his gaze wander over the narrow pit they sat in. Other men were pacing back and forth, some sitting in corners watch the sky fearfully and others cleaning their weapons while waiting for something to happen.

Etakai waited, but Charles never finished his sentence.

"Charles?" Etakai asked, moving to his knees.

Charles shook his head. "I shouldn't panic." He cleared his throat. "You see, after all the explosions communication with HQ. has been completely cut-off. We're a sitting duck."

"You mean we have no orders?" Etakai whispered, knowing better than to shout such a thing when so many men were at that moment willing to run away.

"Our last orders were to stand our ground and wait for further instruction," he murmured, placing a hand over his mouth when some men glanced in their direction. They all knew Charles was in charge and some of them might have been able to read lips. Charles coughed to hide his cover-up and glanced at Etakai. "What I just told you is classified, understand?"

Etakai nodded, but then let his eyes wander to the

sky again.

Two months. How much time had passed in Reitrin's world?

The name brought a sharp stab of regret and Etakai hunched forward, placing his hand over his eyes. He heard Charles ask if he was all right, but Etakai couldn't answer. He wasn't all right.

He was lost in the story with no way to get out and no reason to be there. Not only that but he had abandoned Reitrin to her death.

An explosion went off nearby and Etakai jumped. This time there was gunfire and shouting. Etakai gritted his teeth.

The shooting lasted for hours. A charge was formed, but Etakai was ordered to guard the pit. He was to shoot anyone who appeared at the top of the pit, whether it is friend or foe. Etakai thought that was too cruel. If one of their own men ran back from the charge then why should he shoot them?

Etakai stood staring at the sky, wincing when he heard screams or explosions. The guns fired rapidly back and forth and Etakai nearly dropped his gun when someone ran back to the pit, but was shot down at the edge. He fell into the pit, tumbling to the bottom where he writhed on the ground for a second before becoming limp.

With a dry throat, Etakai looked back up at the top of the barricade. He couldn't stop his heart from racing in his chest, causing his breath to come in sharp gasps. This was nothing like he'd ever seen before. Yes, he had been in plenty of battles; skirmishes between different countries, feuds in villages, and simple raids. This Real World war was a nightmare.

Another person appeared at the top of the barricade. Etakai held up the rifle, but he froze.

The man stood there, panting with blood splattered on his face. His arm was cut open, probably from barbed wire. He was a friend.

Etakai lowered the gun.

The man looked over his shoulder, but then leaped down into the pit and raced past Etakai.

Etakai closed his eyes, his stomach turned in guilt and his chest ached. He couldn't take this. He needed to get away. The war wasn't even his.

Someone else appeared above the barricade.

It was an enemy soldier.

Etakai shot him down. As the man fell to the ground Etakai inhaled sharp. If he had managed to make it to the barricade then that meant …

Etakai shouldered his rifle and climbed the ladder. He caught his breath when he reached the top and found the enemy army running at the barricade.

They had lost.

Etakai leaped back into the pit, racing in the direction the other man had gone. He wasn't sure where he would go. He didn't know this land, but he at least knew where the enemies were.

Shouting rose behind him with more gunfire. He ducked when he heard it rattling against the walls behind him. The sandbags that lined the path burst open and wood splintered, flying in every direction.

Etakai held his hands over his head and ran faster. He could see the exit, but he knew he wouldn't reach it in time. Enemy soldiers appeared in the path behind him.

"Wait, you idiot," Etakai hissed as he ran. "Since when are you tied down to the laws of the Real World?" Etakai cursed his foolishness.

He leaped straight into the air.

Behind him he heard the shouting of the enemy cut off.

Etakai landed on the wall of the barricade and continued to run.

He jumped off the wall onto the flat ground and took off through the maze of barbed wire. There were dead bodies lying everywhere. Etakai held his breath so not to smell the rotting flesh. He splashed through mud puddles and avoided the barbed wire and land mines. The men had been told where the minefield was, but still a few mines had been placed behind their lines in case of a rear attack, which was exactly what happened.

Judging by the black marks on the ground it seemed some of the landmines had blown, but not all. Etakai dodged them, able to hear the faint hum of the mines that other humans would not notice.

Etakai had a stitch in his side from hunger, thirst, and exhaustion. He placed a hand on his side, but then a lump of dread rose to his throat.

It wasn't a stitch in his side at all.

He had been shot.

Blood seeped between his fingers, but he couldn't risk stopping. The enemy was still after him. He could hear them.

Etakai raced into the forest in hope of finding a place to hide. Even in his escape of certain death he hoped Charles was safe. He knew such a hope was futile.

As if on cue, the clouds broke and it began to rain. Etakai kept moving. The pain in his side grew worse.

Etakai slowed to a stop and looked over his shoulder. He was out of breath and, for the moment, out of danger. He leaned forward, grabbing his knees and panting.

"I'm useless," he whispered, holding his bleeding side as he leaned against a tree. "I'm only fooling myself." Etakai sank to the ground and stretched his legs out in front of himself, wincing when his left leg began to cramp. Carefully he rolled up his shirt to check the wound.

It was only a cut. The bullet had nicked his side. Etakai sat back with his eyes closed. Thunder rolled above his head and he blinked in surprise.

The storm was familiar.

"No, I must just be tired," he muttered to the rain. He closed his eyes to get a moment of rest. His stomach ached with hunger and his head spun from exhaustion.

He became aware of the footsteps coming up behind him too late.

His tired gaze examined the people in front of him. They were dressed in navy blue uniforms and were armed.

Etakai shouted when a noose dropped around his neck and wrenched him back against the tree.

It was an attempt to knock him out. Etakai forced himself forward, despite the rope choking him, and grabbed the legs of the man who stood in front of him.

The soldier held his rifle to Etakai's head.

"Let my leg go and sit back like a good boy," said the man, his brown eyes narrowed and his head shaved beneath his hat. He was young.

Etakai moved back, sitting on his feet and glancing over his shoulder at the second man who held the rope.

His head was also buzzed, but he was a little older with hazel eyes. He was taller with a stable build.

Etakai examined them, trying to remember what he had been taught to do when surrounded. He remembered and slowly lifted his hands in the air, placing them on his head.

"Using a rope to capture me is rather barbaric," he told the man in front if him. His voice was hoarse. "I'll go with you willingly if you remove it."

The taller man looked at the other who caught his gaze. He didn't lower the gun from Etakai's forehead.

The short man nodded and Etakai felt a moment of relief. The man behind him removed the rope and instead pulled down Etakai's hands behind his back and tied them.

"Another civilian recruited unwillingly," said the tall man, looking up at the first. "He looks more lost than the other ones we caught."

"I'm thinking he was in the battle back there," murmured the first, examining Etakai slowly. "He's covered in soot and mud. We'll take him to the camp and see what the officers want to do with him."

The taller man grabbed Etakai's bound hands and pulled him to his feet. Etakai flinched when his body protested. It wanted to lie down and sleep, but Etakai knew that wasn't going to happen. The tall man jabbed him in the back with the barrel of his rifle.

"Get moving."

Etakai reluctantly obeyed. The shorter man walked beside him, adjusting his hat as they went. He seemed calm, but Etakai sensed the constant fear that all men in this world felt.

Chapter Fifteen
True Hiro

Reitrin appeared in the midst of a thick forest. The air stank of burning flesh and old wood. She gagged on the stench. The injury in her abdominal seared in pain and she sank to her knees. She glanced around before changing into the clothes she had taken with her. Jeans and a sweater with socks and her shoes. She threw aside the hospital gown and then took the belt Aoiro had given her.

She carefully removed the bandages from her abdomen. The puncture wound began to bleed as she wrapped the belt around the injury. The soft inside was like airy cotton against her skin. It cooled the wound and caressed it gingerly. As she tightened the belt her pain decreased until it was hardly noticeable. She strapped it shut and pulled her shirt over it. The belt hugged her body so there were no odd lumps visible beneath her shirt.

Reitrin walked in a circle then jumped up and down a few times, testing to see how well the belt worked. Her movement caused a tingling sensation in her abdomen, but the pain remained absent.

The stench of smoke had grown heavier and she shuddered. She did not want to know what was being burned. It was twilight and the smoke that hung between the tree branches made it hard to see.

Her gaze swept her surroundings and she began to wonder where to go. She didn't have magical powers to help her hunt down Etakai. All she had was her knowledge of how much trouble he got into. Knowing him he was involved with the stench. Reitrin prayed he wasn't, but she knew he was drawn to trouble, and the smoke stank of trouble.

"Fine," muttered Reitrin. She took her old bandages and wrapped them around her mouth and nose so not to inhale too much smoke. She began her walk through the trees heading into the breeze. The smell grew stronger and the smoke thickened. Reitrin blinked it out of her eyes and searched for its source.

The trees opened up and Reitrin found herself staring into a giant war zone. There were fences of barbed wire, men in informs, large black craters from explosives, and a giant bonfire. On closer inspection Reitrin saw the fire was made of dead bodies.

She shuddered and sank down between the trees, pressing her hand over her nose and mouth. She wanted to vomit.

There were tree stumps all through the area. Reitrin realized the forest had reached farther, but the war cut it back. The wood was used to build the barricades that had sheltered the soldiers now piling their enemy's corpses onto the fire. The flames roared hungrily and Reitrin moved back farther.

A click behind her made her freeze.

"What's this?" It was a deep voice that came from behind her. "Looks like a lost mouse."

Reitrin swallowed hard, slowly lifted her hands and looked over her shoulder. The person was dressed in black with a hood and full face mask. He held the nose of his pistol to Reitrin's head and she stared up the short barrel to the gloves the man wore.

"Stand up slowly," said the man.

Reitrin did as she was told. She cautiously straightened up. The man stepped forward and removed the bandages from her face, tossing them aside. He tilted his head as he examined her. "Who are you?"

"I'm a civilian," said Reitrin, trying to keep her voice steady. "What are you? You don't look like a soldier."

"I'm with a special force," replied the man. He spoke with little emotion. "How did a civilian like you make it out here? They were cleared out days ago just in case the army needed to use its secret weapon."

"Secret weapon?" Reitrin asked, raising an eyebrow at the man. "I don't remember–" She cut off and looked over her shoulder, pretending to have heard something. She had been about to tell him that she'd never read about a secret weapon. There was noting written about it in real history books. Maybe it was something the author had concocted for the story?

"I think it was just a bird," muttered Reitrin, looking back at the man. "We weren't told why the soldiers made us evacuate. I didn't know there was a secret weapon."

"Of course you wouldn't. It's secret for a reason. Are you so dense?"

"I'm a little shaken," replied Reitrin hotly. "I got lost in the woods–"

"Why are you exploring the woods during a war?"

"My friend is missing," replied Reitrin, lowering her voice and looking away. The man would not take her seriously if she did not act as if her missing friend were not direly important to her. She swallowed hard and looked at her hands as she whispered, "My fiancé went missing when we were evacuated. When he never returned I decided to search for him. I know it sounds stupid. I mean, what chance do I have of ever finding him?" She bit her lip and felt tears welling up in her eyes. The foul smoke made them come easy. Reitrin hoped her act was good enough.

The soldier watched her for a moment, but then lowered his pistol. "What's your fiancé's name? He may have been taken and enlisted to fight."

Reitrin gave him a startled look. "What?" Her eyes jumped to the pile of dead bodies.

"Only our enemies are in that fire," said the soldier. "If we took your fiancé then he will be among those we were burying all day." He pointed across the battle field to where there were hundreds of dirt mounds. "Unless he still lives, but if that is the case I will know who he is when you tell me his name. I know the names of all survivors."

Reitrin cast a wary glance at the fire once more. "Etakai. His name is Etakai."

The soldier was motionless, but then shook his head. "I don't know that name."

Reitrin's shoulders slumped. She knew she had been hoping for too much.

"Perhaps he was captured by the enemy and made to fight with them," said the soldier. "We captured a few of their men and they will soon be sent to a holding camp. I can let you speak to them if you would like." He looked down at Reitrin who was staring at him.

"Would you?" She whispered.

"Yes," replied the soldier. "But keep in mind that if they do not know of him either then chances are he is long dead."

"I just need to know," Reitrin whispered, wiping a tear from her cheek. "I just … I just need to know." She sniffed as more tears ran down her face.

"We can't waste time here," said the soldier, reaching into his jacket. "You're lucky I'm the one that found you. Had my captain stumbled upon you you'd be dead by now." He withdrew a rag and passed it to Reitrin who dabbed at her face. The rag was surprisingly clean for having come from a worn out soldier.

"This way," said the soldier, motioning her down towards the camp. "I will escort you to the cage and there you can speak to the prisoners."

"Okay," whispered Reitrin. She hurried after him, but he linked elbows with her and looked down at her.

"Don't tell me your name," he whispered in her ear. "No matter who speaks to you, please use a fake name."

"Why?" Reitrin was alarmed.

"I am cursed," replied the man. "Anyone whose name I learn dies a terrible death and I am always present. So please do not speak your name, understood?"

"Okay," said Reitrin, feeling frightened. "But I told you my fiancé's name."

"He will be fine as long as I never meet him," replied the man.

Reitrin glanced at the mask the man wore. His

arm linked with hers felt surprisingly hard and Reitrin was reminded of someone else; a man who was more machine, emotionless, yet kind. Her curiosity pulled the question from her lips before she could stop it.

"Are you named Hiro?"

The man stopped dead in his tracks. He rounded on her, pulling the mask from his face. His golden eyes were wide with horror and his pale skin was so white it put snow to shame.

It was him.

"How do you know that name?" Hiro whispered, his voice cracking from fright. "No one except the scientists knows my real name."

Reitrin gawked at him. "I've met you before. Only I met you in a different story."

Hiro became emotionless. "Story? Are you speaking of magic?"

"Something like that," muttered Reitrin. "It's hard to explain, but I am here to find my friend and leave. If you can help me I'll explain everything to you, but I don't think you'll believe me."

Hiro looked around them. They had stopped amidst the battle ground. The fences of barbed wire were near and the smog of smoke lingered above their heads.

"There is not much I do not believe," Hiro said. He rolled up his shirt, revealing an abdomen made of steel. The thin wires and carefully crafted angles were beautiful and Reitrin stared.

"I was supposed to be an emotionless weapon," Hiro explained, lowering his shirt. "I am the secret weapon I told you about."

Reitrin could only stare at Hiro. The man before

her looked no younger than the Hiro she met in *Blood River*. Had Aoiro placed him here? Or was this his story?

There was something strange going on.

"What was I like in this other story?" Hiro looked at her with no sign of curiosity. In fact, now that his fear had subsided, he looked careless. It reminded Reitrin of Etakai.

"I don't think I should tell you," said Reitrin, frowning. "It might have a negative effect on what you turn into if you hear about your other self from me. I don't think it's worth the risk."

Hiro looked away.

"Can we speak to the prisoners now?" Reitrin asked, hoping to change the subject.

Hiro was motionless, but then nodded once. He led her in the direction of the barricade.

"Am I a monster in the future?" he asked quietly.

"I can't say for sure," she muttered. "But I don't think you were a monster."

Hiro was still emotionless, but Reitrin wondered if she had seen a peaceful expression cross his face.

Chapter Sixteen
Only One Choice

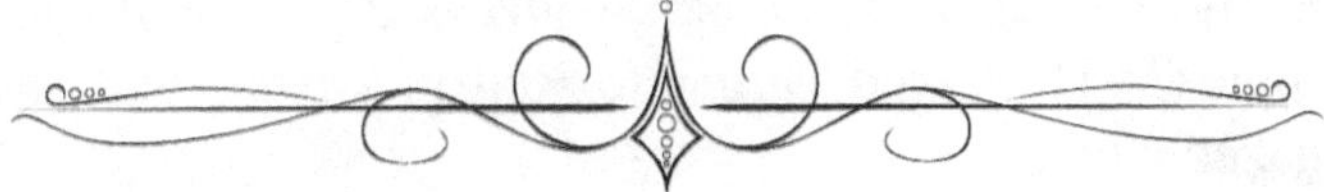

The prisoners were being kept in a cage that stood in the midst of the field surrounded by mud. Inside the cage the men were caked in mud and blood. Not all of them had bandages and most had torn their clothes to bind their wounds. All eyes turned to Hiro and Reitrin as they approached.

"What's this?" One asked, looking up at Hiro with cold humor. "Come to feed the starving dogs a little girl?"

"Humans should not eat human flesh," said Hiro.

"Machines should not speak like people," the man retorted.

Hiro did not answer. "The lady is seeking someone from your company. Her fiancé. She wishes to speak to you to see if any of you know of him."

"None of us in here would mind passing as her fiancé," laughed a rude man in the back.

"Please, listen," said Reitrin, stepping forward. "His name is Etakai. He has hair like silver and different colored eyes–" She was interrupted by the first man whose blue eyes lit up at her description.

"Etakai?" He repeated, rolling onto his knees and grabbing the cage bars. "You are a friend of Etakai's?"

Reitrin's heart jumped. "You know him?"

"I found him wandering lost in the heat of battle," explained the man. "I took care of him. The man was unsure of everything out here. I taught him to fire a gun, and always tried to make him laugh, yet not once did a smile touch his lips. He spoke of bad memories when he spoke at all. Are you really his fiancé?" He stared hard into Reitrin's eyes, and she gazed back.

Reitrin did not want to lie to this man. "Who are you?"

"I'm called Charles," the man replied. "And you?"

Reitrin glanced at Hiro who shrugged and covered his ears.

"I'm Reitrin." She approached the cage so she and Charles could speak quietly. The other men were watching with interest. It seemed they all knew Etakai and wondered who Reitrin was.

"You're quite a risk taker," whispered Charles. "Claiming to be Etakai's fiancé. I know he had no such lover."

"It's a good story to get where I need to," replied Reitrin quietly. "I came to find him. He's in danger."

"I'd say," grumbled Charles. "I may not know Etakai well, but I'm certain he escaped the war and made a break for the forest. He would always mutter under his breath about how much he preferred the forest to open areas."

"Do you think Etakai is alive?" Reitrin asked. "Do you know any way I can find him?"

"Instinct?" Charles suggested. "Etakai wouldn't let himself die. He's a stubborn brute. I know he's out there somewhere and I hope you find him, but I can't help you."

Hiro lowered his hands from his ears. "Time is up. I need to escort you off the premises before my captain finds you."

"Okay," muttered Reitrin. She thanked Charles and turned to Hiro, but before she could say a word her eyes landed on a stranger who was standing a few steps behind Hiro. He wore a black uniform and had short brown hair with a hat.

Reitrin knew at once that he was trouble.

"Hirochi," said the man, making Hiro look back. "Who is that?"

"A civilian looking for her fiancé," replied Hiro. He was not alarmed by the stranger. "I am going to escort her off the premises since the man she seeks is not among the prisoners."

"No, bring her to my tent," replied the man.

Hiro saluted and the man walked away.

Reitrin watched the man. Whoever he was, Reitrin could tell he was not a normal soldier.

"Are we in trouble?" Reitrin whispered as Hiro took her arm to lead her.

"Yes," replied Hiro. "I'm afraid we are."

Hiro led Reitrin after the man. They crossed to a row of tents and followed the man into the tallest.

Inside there was a desk, an oil lamp, a collection of weapons beside the desk, and maps, ink, and parchment on the desk. The man dropped into a seat behind the desk and removed his hat, tossing it onto the desk.

"What do you think you're doing, Hiro?" the man inquired slyly. "Seeing you beside a woman is a little frightening."

Hiro said nothing.

"The scientists let you wander the area freely to test your loyalty to the mission and your discipline," continued the man. "I am not saying that assisting a civilian is a sign of disloyalty, but not bringing her to me first is not acceptable. However, since you are not accustomed to being around civilians I am going to let this slide without reporting it."

Hiro was still silent.

Reitrin wasn't sure if he was scared or simply did not want to show gratitude for the kindness he was being shown. She looked at him, then back at the man whose bronze eyes landed on her.

"What is your name?" The man asked.

Reitrin hesitated. She couldn't think of a fake name. "Given the circumstances, I think you should tell me who you are first."

The man's eyebrows shot up, but then he grinned. "I suppose that would be more polite since you are the lady here and in a more honorable position, being a civilian." The way he said this sounded both polite and spiteful. "I am Gechio, posing as captain and Hiro's retainer."

"Retainer," Reitrin repeated quietly. She glanced at Hiro again. Was he that dangerous?

"Now, who are you?" Gechio's voice had no kindness as he leaned forward with his elbows on the desk.

"R – Ray," she stammered, her face blushed. It was the same name she had told Aoiro in *Blood River* and she was embarrassed that she had used it yet again, even after Aoiro told her how lame it was.

"I hope that wasn't your real name," Gechio chuckled. "If it is then you'll die an awful death with Hiro by your side."

"I don't get the joke," Reitrin said, playing dumb.

"Never mind," replied Gechio, waving a hand at her. "What brings you to this area?"

Reitrin explained the same story she had told Hiro, making sure to look as grievous as she could manage. "It seems like he was never here, though," Reitrin muttered in the end. "No one knows of him."

"Pity," said Gechio, though there was only apathy in his tone. "Well now, you're in this a little too deep, girl."

"What do you mean?"

"You know Hiro is a weapon," replied Gechio plainly. "Either we have to kill you or force you to work for us."

"What?" Reitrin demanded.

"Oddly sweet of you, Gechio," Hiro finally spoke up. "Offering her life? Are you taken by her?"

"Shut up," said Gechio, tossing a pen at Hiro who caught it and set it back on the desk.

"She should be returned to her home," Hiro said. "Why keep her here under a death threat?"

"It's a real threat," replied Gechio. "I was told that if anyone found out what you are they need to be killed."

Hiro offered no reply.

"So," said Gechio to Reitrin. "What will it be?"

Reitrin already knew her answer. Death was not an option, but she had a feeling her situation could work out in her favor. "I'm not very strong, but if it means I won't be killed I would like to help you. I may find my fiancé this way."

"I doubt that," said Gechio, rising to his feet. "You'll be under constant surveillance because I think you're lying, Ray." He grinned at her and then looked at Hiro. "Take her to the supplies tent and find her something to wear. Don't let her escape. I know you can do that without difficulty, so if she manages to escape I will hunt her down and kill her. Do you understand? She is your responsibility and will be killed if she leaves your side."

Hiro saluted. "Understood." He turned, took Reitrin's arm, and left the tent.

Reitrin took a last glance at Gechio over her shoulder. When she met his eye she saw there was nothing but emptiness as he watched her. Reitrin realized he was just as much a machine as Hiro.

Chapter Seventeen
Etakai's Peril

The light bulb swayed from the rumble of thunder and pound of rain. Men groaned, some coughed, others gasped as if they could not remember how to breathe. Night was always this way. The barracks smelled of sweat, blood, and other unpleasant aroma. The beds were cramped and so were the floors. The men had to sleep pushed up against one another for warmth and space. So many men were crammed into one barrack that often times groups were walked out by the guards and never seen again.

The light went out and silence fell. It was time to sleep. With the moaning and coughing of sick men and retched smells it was near impossible to doze off. It was especially hard for Etakai, who sat in the farthest corner from the door.

His arms were crossed, his head down, and his eyes shut. He wore shabby gray pants and matching baggy shirt. His worn boots remained on his feet and were coated in dry mud. His head was buzzed and he wore a hat with a bill to shade his eyes. A filthy cloth was wrapped around his head to cover his left eye.

His eye opened to look at the old man at his feet. Etakai's blue eye narrowed and he cursed under his breath. The old man had died. Etakai pushed the corpse away with his foot and withdrew to the corner.

He wrapped his arms around his body to try warming himself, but the room was like ice. Mist came from his nose when he exhaled. No matter how cold he was he could not curl up with the mass of warm bodies. The only human who had offered warmth was the old man now dead at his feet. It was not pride that kept him in the corner; it was fear.

The men in the barrack could turn hostile at any minute. There were guards outside the barracks, listening for sounds of commotion. Fists thrown meant shots fired; the smell of blood lingered from such nights. Etakai wanted to avoid fights at all cost. He feared the men, but he also pitied them. The story they had been written into was dreadful.

They had suffered in the camp for months. He had been captured several weeks ago, but already he felt the agony of an empty stomach, a weak body, harassment and embarrassment. He could only imagine how terrible it was for those around him. Many were men who had been taken from their families. Others had watched members of their family being shot and killed. Some cases were worse than a simple death and Etakai shuddered.

The stories he heard plagued him.

He lifted his head, listening to the footfalls of a soldier patrolling the barrack outside. He clenched his jaw and hoped the doors would not open. It was in the middle of the night when the soldiers came in, selected a large number of men, and took them away.

"Hey," whispered a voice from a bunk beside the corner.

Etakai glanced up.

Above him there was a scraggly young boy who looked as if he had not eaten in weeks. He waved and placed his fingers to his lips. This was pointless since

Etakai did not wish to speak.

"What are you?" The boy whispered.

Etakai arched an eyebrow. "What am I?"

"Your hair was pretty before they shaved it off," the boy whispered. "Long and silver, but you're not old enough to have gray hair."

"I am peculiar," replied Etakai.

Someone in the room began to snore and the boy jumped, looking around. They were silent for a moment, but then the boy looked back down at Etakai. "My name is Shilo. What's yours?"

Etakai held the boy's gaze. He couldn't ignore it. His pity for the poor starved boy was growing. With everything they had to go through he felt his heart ache just seeing the hope in the boy's eyes.

"Etakai," he said gently. "My name is Etakai."

The boy smiled. "I think you're a strong person. I want to be your friend."

Etakai shook his head. "My friends end up dead. You don't want to be one of them."

Shilo became solemn. "But you look like you could save anyone."

Etakai flinched at his words. "I'm … not much good at heroism." He gazed at the dead man by his feet. His thoughts went to Reitrin and the sword that had pierced her. "In fact … I'm rather hopeless."

"You don't sleep," said the boy. "You listen for the guards every night. You watch everyone and you purposefully get between soldiers and the men they plan to harm. I've seen you take beatings for twelve men so far without them even knowing they were in trouble."

Etakai could have laughed. The boy had been

watching him for quite a while. "Don't tell anyone. Even in a place like this, a man holds to what little pride he has." Etakai lowered his head to his chest, holding himself tighter. "Even though they try so hard to take everything we are. If we lose our pride, we are as good as dead. It will not go well if the men know I have been helping them survive."

The boy frowned at the sorrow in Etakai's voice. "Why do you do it? There is nothing worth living for in this camp. Most of us no longer have families or friends to see again. I know a lot of us want to die."

Etakai opened his mouth, but words didn't come. He bowed his head, his blue eye misting over. "I had a friend. I don't often make friends, but … I respected her."

"What happened?"

Etakai passed his hand over his face. "I couldn't protect her. Because of me … she was hurt fatally. I left before I knew if she would make it, but I am sure she is long dead. I've been gone for so long."

The boy frowned. Stories like this were common in the camp. "How was she hurt?"

"No." Etakai cast the boy a cold look. "Go to sleep. You need rest."

The boy hunched his shoulders, but then sank out of sight.

Etakai gritted his teeth and griped his arms harder. He couldn't shake the memories. Seeing Flamelord's sword cut through the air and Reitrin running to take the blade. That was the kind of hero he was supposed to be. It should not have been Reitrin taking the hit. Etakai should have been the one to die.

All he did was fail. And now he lived in grief.

It was his fault she was gone.

"I'm sorry," whispered Etakai, placing his hands over his face. "I'm so sorry, Reitrin."

Chapter Eighteen
Their Plan

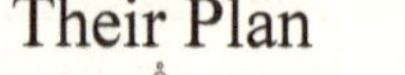

Hiro and Gechio told her they were erasers. Gechio was constantly at Hiro's side while they traveled and the normal soldiers trailed behind them like stray dogs. There was a horse-drawn cart with the prisoners chained up upon it in a large cage with an old tarp over top. Hiro and Gechio were assigned to the caravan to make sure they arrived at their destination safely.

It was slow going through the mud and rain and the horses would slip and injure themselves on the slopes. Already they had to put down two of the noble animals.

Reitrin saw the men put a bullet though the head of each injured horse. It twisted her stomach. Yes, it was an act of mercy, but her heart ached when they leashed up a new horse and headed out, leaving the dead ones on the side of the road to rot.

There was no time to linger since they were in enemy territory.

Reitrin marched with the men, her hair cut even shorter than it had been before. She wore a hat and could have been mistaken for a young man with all the dirt on her face.

Their first day marching, Reitrin had fallen in line near the back. It was only a few minutes in before Hiro stopped the company and called her to the front.

This brought stares from the soldiers as well as the prisoners.

Reitrin hurried to obey the eraser. He had her walk between him and Gechio and the company moved out again. This made Reitrin feel unsettled. Only captains or those in command were supposed to be up front. What was going on?

Some of the soldiers traveling behind them would nudge each other and whisper about her behind her back, but she was unaware of what they said. She guessed it was repulsive because one time Hiro had stopped in his tracks when he heard them and looked at the men.

Though there was no emotion, the look shut the men up at once. After that they remained silent.

Reitrin was bewildered. Hiro said he had no emotions, but he acted as if he knew right from wrong and in his own way he was looking out for her. Maybe he was still human deep down inside, but there was no real way of knowing. When she felt the steel beneath his arms and heard the mechanical whining in his joints she quickly forgot his moments of human acts.

In the afternoon the company came to a halt. A short break to check the perimeter and tend to the prisoners.

Gechio pulled out a map and turned to Reitrin and Hiro. "Part one worked fine." He spoke under his breath, pretending to be discussing the map.

Reitrin gave him a bewildered look.

"Gechio wants to help you," Hiro explained.

"What?" Reitrin was surprised.

"He has a soft spot for women."

"Shut up, I do not." Gechio shot Hiro a glare. He then looked at Reitrin. "It is not in my power to ensure your safety. You see, Hiro and I will have to leave you guys in a few months. He and I have been ordered to a new mission. The prisoners in this caravan are to be sent to a holding camp. The soldiers will also be housed there until further notice. That means you, too."

Reitrin stared at him. There was no way she would survive with a group of soldiers who hadn't seen a woman in months. Reitrin looked at Hiro who avoided her gaze.

"We are not to bring any of the soldiers with us when we depart," Gechio added. "If you came with us you would be in more danger than with these men."

"He does care," Hiro said.

"Shut it," Gechio snapped.

"Why help me?" Reitrin asked.

"It's Hiro's fault," Gechio muttered to the map. "He won't stop dropping subtle hints that he thinks we ought to help you."

Reitrin stared at Hiro who was watching the men resting their feet or tending to the horses.

"Hiro doesn't feel anything, so the fact that he's determined to help you tells me it should be worth our time," Gechio concluded. "We have to move out now. You'll be sticking with us from here on out."

"Okay. Uh, sir." Reitrin added the last part awkwardly and gave him a puzzled look.

"We'll work on it," Gechio said, folding up the map. "Hiro, ready the men. We head out in ten minutes."

Hiro nodded and left them.

When he was gone Gechio looked down at Reitrin. "You're job from here is to make sure the men recognize you as an authority. That is the only way they'll leave you alone."

Reitrin gave a start. "But I'm not–"

"A man or a captain," Gechio finished. He nodded. "We have a few months to work on that."

"Why are you helping me, really?" Reitrin directed this question with suspicion. "You were the one who wanted me dead. I don't see Hiro actually managing to change your mind."

Gechio opened his mouth, but then shut it with a shrug. "He's right that I can't resist a pretty face. And yours is quite lovely, despite the dirt."

Reitrin gawked at him.

"Don't speak of any of this unless Hiro or I bring it up first," Gechio warned. "Act as we instruct. We don't need the men to catch on."

"Yes, sir," said Reitrin with a curt nod.

"Good," said Gechio. "Remember, you have to earn respect, not demand it."

Reitrin nodded again. This was going to be a pain.

The company set out again. Reitrin stayed ahead with Gechio and Hiro. Back and forth the two shot small notes to her, like, "Straighten your back," or, "Look straight ahead." Reitrin made these small adjustments, wondering if it looked odd to the company of men trailing them.

It was likely they were too focused on their mission though. They were marching through enemy territory and Reitrin had to keep this in mind as well.

When night fell each man was responsible for pitching their own tent, and Reitrin was no exception. That night it was raining and the mud was slippery, but Reitrin had little difficulty managing the simple structure of the tent.

She felt the soldiers watching her as she hammered the stakes into the ground. When she glanced around she met their gaze as Gechio had instructed.

"Hold their gaze," Gechio told her. "Don't speak. Wasting words will do you no good. And don't smile or glare. Appear indifferent."

It was difficult. She wanted to glare when the men snickered behind their hands or pointed at her. Reitrin looked away, finishing her work. The prisoners were kept in the middle of camp and taken out in turns to relieve themselves. Reitrin's tent was far from the prisoners. Gechio requested this, since Reitrin had spoke to the prisoners. He didn't want them on friendly terms.

When the camp was set, the men gathered in the center of the encampment where Hiro and Gechio did a roll-call to make sure no one had fallen behind. They selected men for the first watch, and gave out a brief update on their progress. After that the men were excused to rest.

This would be their nightly routine and as Reitrin retired to her tent she wondered if Gechio would make her take roll-call eventually.

Raindrops pitter-pattered on the roof of the white tents that evening. It had been one day, but Reitrin ached all over.

A leak seeped through the roof and she watched as the water slithered down the cloth and formed a puddle in the corner. The grass was slurping the water, but not fast enough. The sleeping bag Reitrin laid out was thin with a musty smell. She knew she would be getting no sleep.

Reitrin shut her eyes. She breathed in the scent of rain and damp fabric. She was no closer to finding Etakai than she had been before. She pulled off the damp navy blue jacket and sat in the plain gray t-shirt and pants. Her boots were set near the door, but she kept her socks on. Since she was alone, she lifted her shirt to check the belt she wore.

She managed to keep it dry. The constant rain made her uneasy. Thankfully, the jackets of the uniform repelled the rain well. Reitrin rolled her shirt back down and sat silently.

How was she supposed to sleep with an army of potentially desperate men outside her tent? Not only that, but every moment they spent immobile was another moment Etakai could be moving farther away.

Reitrin wished she knew some way to locate him. The story may have been historical, but it was still fiction, so perhaps she could find a way?

Sighing, Reitrin laid down and shut her eyes. More than anything she wished she could take a long hot shower.

Chapter Nineteen
The Holding Camp

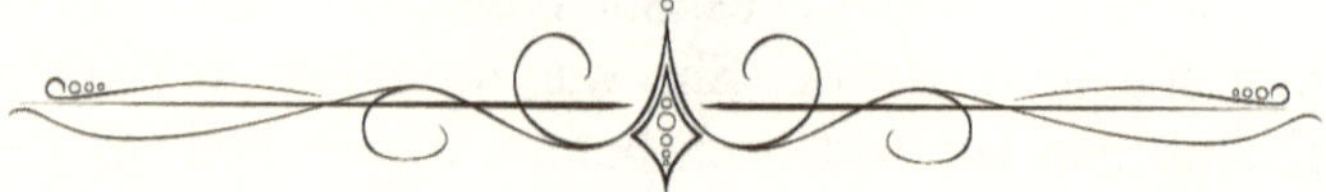

The pouring rain made life worse. Digging graves and building new barracks in ankle-deep mud slowed the process. It gave their guards reason to shout at them, beat them, and push them around. Even the young boys were shown no mercy. They did what they could, but there was no way they could match the pace of the full-grown men they were compared to. They struggled and Shilo was knocked down by a guard who shouted at him to stop being weak. The boy was trying not to cry and the soldier lifted his gun to beat him.

His gun was seized from behind. He looked back and met the stern glare of Etakai. His blue eye appeared to glow with menace.

"I'll complete the boys work load as well as my own," he said in a dangerous voice. "So don't harm him or he will be even more useless."

The soldier shoved Etakai away with a scowl. "Have it your way." He kicked Shilo down then marched off.

"You shouldn't have done that," said Shilo, pulling himself out of the mud.

"I'm already a target," said Etakai. He helped the boy to stand and retrieved his shovel.

"Thank you," whispered Shilo as he continued to dig the post hole for the new barrack.

"We need to pick up the pace if we're to keep out of trouble," muttered Etakai. The rain was making everyone groggy, but they had to meet their daily expectations or they would be denied dinner.

The Real World was a miserable place deep in its roots. Etakai wondered how accurate the camp was. Had people in this world been treated like this for real? Or was it amplified for the sake of a story line?

He would not learn the answer unless he could escape the book.

The rain grew harder, but the prisoners were forced to keep working. Etakai and the other men were shouting to one another over the pouring rain as they set the posts and began to lift the walls into place. They were slipping in the mud and one boy nearly fell on his face in the mud. Etakai caught the back of his shirt and pulled him up, all the while keeping a hold of the wall so it wouldn't fall. He was true to his word and did both his work and the work of Shilo.

It was not unusual for him to get between a guard and prisoner, but up until that day he hadn't spoken to the guards. He had a bad feeling about it. By lunch he knew the guards and prisoners would know about the exchange. He kept his head down for the rest of the day so not to risk drawing more trouble to him and Shilo.

Night fell and the security lights flickered on, signaling it was time for them to return to their barracks. Etakai and the others marched through the mud onto the stone paths that led to their barracks. Etakai felt guards and prisoners watching him as he passed them. He was the first into the barrack. As soon as he collapsed into his corner Shilo was there, but he was not alone.

"You're in deep, my friend," said an older man who had once been strong and toned, but was now skin and bones. "No one speaks to a guard like that and gets away with it."

"I know," said Etakai. "I probably caused another walk-out tonight."

Some of the men cast nervous looks to the door as more of their barrack members entered. There was much murmuring as they spoke of what Etakai had done, though none knew his name. They called him by the number on his clothes; Number 0637. It was how most of them knew each other. Rarely did they learn names.

"I don't foresee another walk-out," sighed the old man, sitting down at Etakai's side. "But you may be taken aside and 'talked to,' if you catch my drift."

"All too clearly," replied Etakai grimly.

Shilo rested his forehead on Etakai's knee, shutting his eyes. Etakai frowned at him, but did not push him away. Other men came and asked for more details on what had happened. It had been a short occurrence, but it was the only thing the men talked about. All night Etakai saw men glancing at him. He was not sure how much worse it could get.

Shilo and the old man fell asleep on either side of him and for the first time in a long time, Etakai felt needed. He was surrounded by people that did not want him to be taken away. If another walk-out were to happen he would step up and go so the others wouldn't have to, but that would not save anyone for longer than a few days.

He remembered then that Fevros had offered to free him if he became a loyal servant. Etakai cursed the man and his smug smile. Fevros had let an entire world die without batting an eye. He would not care if the same fate befell Etakai in this land.

Etakai would save the men, but to do that he would need to get them ready to fight. They were weak and outnumbered. Such a plan would end in more than half the prisoners being shot and killed. Etakai had not wanted to risk their lives, which was why he had remained silent for so long.

Now he was a target. He would no longer be able to hide in the shadows and keep his head down.

The next day dawned with no walk-outs. The men were woken before dawn by the trumpet and their guards marched them to the building sight they were last at. It was still raining, though not as hard, but there were puddles everywhere. The men worked long past sunrise in the mud and water before the trumpet sounded again. They were marched to the mess hall to get their portion of cold porridge before being sent back to work.

The mess hall was a large building with a tall ceiling and prisoners with trays in a line up either side of the room, which was filled with tables and chairs.

Some prisoners were finishing up and being marched out. As they left the new group filed in and began to fill the seats. The porridge was white and had the texture of mud and frog eggs.

Etakai came up in line the soldier serving the porridge dumped a little in his tray, but then knocked it from his hands.

Some of the men jerked forward to protest, but stopped abruptly.

"Get going," said the soldier, scowling at Etakai.

"That's all you get."

Etakai moved on without a word. He joined Shilo at the table and folded his arms on the table. The embarrassment prickled at the back of his neck.

Shilo slid his bowl towards Etakai who shook his head.

"You'll get in trouble if they see you share with me," Etakai whispered. The last thing he wanted was to make life worse for the boy. Shilo was beaten often.

The meal ended and they were escorted out of the mess hall as the next group entered. Etakai met the eye of each man that happened to look at him. Not many had the will to fight, or to even live. By the time he was outside he knew he would be the topic around their tables.

That was what he hoped for.

Back at work, the guards were hovering closer than usual. The mud and clay made work hazardous and a wall almost fell on one of the young boys. Etakai and two other men caught it in time, pulling it back as the others helped him steady it. The guards shouted at Etakai who ignored them and held the wall in place as the other men hammered it in place.

A rifle butt slammed into Etakai's back and he slipped in the mud, collapsing into a puddle. He picked himself up, but the guards were upon him. They kicked him and hit him with the rifles.

When the pummel ended the guards told him never to ignore a direct order. They walked away and Etakai rose to his knees then got back to work.

Night fell and they were escorted to their barrack. Etakai fell back to walk inside the group of men, which, to his relief, were okay with it. They stayed around him until they were back in the barracks. Etakai returned to his corner, but more then Shilo and the other old man joined him.

"Willingly remaining a target is suicide," said a blond man who was not much older than Etakai. "If they don't get you in a walk-out they'll kill you while we're building."

"Starving me seems to be their goal," said Etakai as he sat in the corner with a yawn.

Shilo placed a piece of bread in Etakai's hand and Etakai looked at it with surprise.

"Starving won't be your problem," said the blond.

"We won't let you starve," explained the older man at Etakai's side.

Etakai glanced at him. The number on his clothes was 4040. The young man before him was 4201. His head was buzzed like every other man in the room. He sank down and looked Etakai in the eye.

"You're not like the rest of us, Zero-Six-Three-Seven," he told Etakai. "You're not threatened by the guards and they've started to notice, as have we. I speak for all of us here when we say you need to keep your head down if you aren't planning on doing something stupid."

"But I am," replied Etakai.

The men of the barrack fell silent at once. Everyone had been pretending not to listen, but now all eyes were on Etakai.

"I won't say anything is going to happen right away," Etakai told them. "But I may as well warn you that recently I decided I don't like it here." A few men chuckled at that. "And so I plan on leaving, but I want to bring as many of you with me as I can."

"To our graves, right?" a wheezy old man called in the back.

"Yours, perhaps," said Etakai, locking the man in a stern stare from across the room. "If you enter into this with half a heart you'll leave in a casket. It's all or nothing, but my plan is not complete, so don't speak to me about it until I bring it up." He looked around the room. "Do we understand each other?"

The men in the room muttered their understanding and nodded their heads.

"Let's not make this more of a scene," said Etakai quietly. He glanced over his shoulder at the wall. He could hear a guard coming near their barrack. "Leave me be, or we may all get walked out."

The men dispersed to their beds or spots on the floor. Shilo and 4040 remained with Etakai. Even 4201 had moved to a position closer to Etakai.

Etakai leaned his head against the wood and listened as a guard moved on. Etakai hoped the guard had not heard anything important. There was little that could be done if he had.

The next morning was not rainy, but the mud and clouds remained. Etakai and the others finished the walls before breakfast. The men were walking with Etakai in the center again so the guards would not get to him. Etakai was denied food again, but it didn't faze him. He sat and looked over the men around him. There was another group from a different barrack on the other side of the room. A few of them were looking in his direction and when they did he met their gaze and held it until they looked away.

The meal ended and they left as the next group entered. Etakai was passing through the door when someone placed a piece of paper in his hand. He pocketed it.

Their group was beginning the laborious work of putting up the roof. It took longer than the sides and was risky. The boys held the ladders and the men stood on walls, creating the frames and placing boards across them. Etakai hammered in nails to attach the planks of wood. From on top of the roof Etakai counted the guards standing by and knew how many men were working on each new barrack. His gaze wandered to the wall and barbed wire where sentry towers stood with search lights every couple of yards. Etakai analyzed everything and made mental notes.

Etakai noticed three guards standing nearer the work zone than usual. When he descended the ladder to get more nails he wasn't surprised when they confronted him.

"Stealing bread from the other inmates, were you?" One demanded, pushing Etakai back from Shilo, who was holding the pail of nails.

Shilo looked alarmed, but Etakai shot him a warning look to keep him away.

"Don't you have anything to say?" The second guard asked, shrugging his rifle from his shoulder.

Etakai didn't answer the guards. He merely watched them, but this put the guards in a worse mood.

"We don't tolerate thieves," The guard said as he moved forward.

Etakai shut his eyes when the rifle landed hard on his shoulder. He lurched down, but then the second rifle stuck the outside of his leg and he crashed to his knees.

The guards pummeled him with blows that hurt, but wouldn't maim. Etakai kept his head down as the blows continued. When the guards finally left Etakai stood up, winced, and went to get the nails from Shilo.

Shilo was speechless as Etakai wiped blood off his shoulder and took a handful of nails from the pail. To Shilo Etakai was either a man that felt no pain or he was the strongest man alive. He was in awe as Etakai climbed back to the roof to continue working.

How was he so brave?

That night the men gathered around Etakai again, but he told them all to keep their heads down and explained the plan wasn't yet formed.

It was a quiet night. Etakai felt drowsy and wondered if he would finally get sleep. He remembered the paper someone had passed him.

He fetched it from his pocket and blinked slowly, letting his blue eye glow gently as he peeled open the sweat-damp note.

It was written on a piece of scrap paper with charcoal so the words were smudged in spots, but Etakai understood the message without problem.

"We are ready for a revolution, Captain," Etakai read softly. He tore it up and shoved the pieces into his boot so it would never be found. "Captain, huh? I never thought I'd end up following in my father's footsteps."

Chapter Twenty
Playing the Part

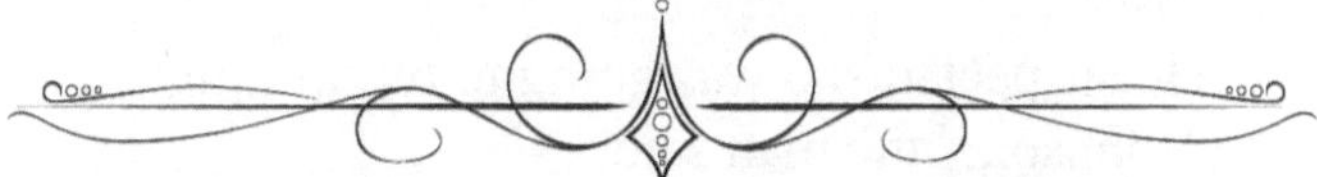

Every morning before the men woke up, Reitrin removed the magazines from her firearms and practiced dry firing. Hiro had shown her how to dismantle and clean her weapons and put them back together. Her morning practice was to take the guns apart, put them back together, and then practiced dry firing until the gun no longer moved in her hands when she pulled the trigger.

Her trigger finger was numb before she stopped for the morning. She reloaded her weapons, making sure the magazines were full, and then pulled on her jacket and buttoned it up. She pushed back her oily hair and pulled on her hat, then left her tent before the sun was up. She tore down her tent, rolled it up, and attached it to the pack she carried along with her sleeping bag.

Every morning the men woke up to find her packed and ready, and on her way to meet with Hiro and Gechio.

One morning, a week into their journey, Reitrin passed by a soldier tearing down his tent.

She heard him mutter, "Pampered bitch."

Reitrin stopped beside him and met his gaze. Gechio had told her to start learning the names of the men. The man that had spoken had thin arms and a face with narrow eyes and a crude smile. Though his name was on his jacket, it was worn and illegible.

"What's your name?" Reitrin asked.

The man looked surprised at first, but then suspicion came over him. He knew she was close to the erasers.

He suspected she was going to report him.

"Johnson," the man said.

"Nice to meet you," said Reitrin. She turned and continued on her way without a backwards glance.

Hiro and Gechio were standing just outside the camp, looking over the map.

"It's been a week," said Gechio as Reitrin approached. "How many names have you learned?"

"I learned a lot of them go by nicknames," Reitrin reported as she joined them. "I think the only real name I've received is Johnson's."

"Likely," said Gechio, nodding as he folded the map. "Hiro recently reported you're the talk of the camp, but not because you're female." He smirked at Reitrin who watched him suspiciously.

"He's happy," Hiro told her.

"Very," Gechio added, grinning. "Twice now the men heard you practicing with your weapons in your tent. Your routine is also helping your reputation. The men won't want to mess with an armed chick who keeps her weaponry close."

"He's upset he didn't think of it," Hiro said.

Gechio glared at the emotionless man.

Reitrin grinned at the two of them. A week of travel with them and she was beginning to get used to them. Gechio was just as emotionless as Hiro, but he did have a soft spot for Reitrin. He treated the men coldly, not speaking to them unless they were messing up formation or weren't wearing their uniform right. How Gechio treated Reitrin really was special.

No wonder she appeared pampered to the men.

"If only we could get you to shoot one of them," Gechio said, rubbing his chin. "Then they'd really be scared of you."

"I'd rather not stoop to the level of an eraser," Reitrin muttered.

Gechio looked offended.

Hiro didn't react.

"I'll report that Johnson called me a foul name," Reitrin said. "So I asked for his name and then left."

"He's a tough cookie," Gechio chuckled.

"Shall we have her shoot him?" Hiro asked.

"You asking that with a straight face is frightening," Gechio said.

They moved out not long after that.

Day by day, Reitrin kept to her routine. She could feel her weak body growing stronger, though she was weary and hungry most of the time. Three weeks passed and she had little trouble handling her weapons. The rifle over her shoulder didn't hurt to carry during the march. The pistol in her belt no longer left blisters from the constant rubbing.

Then there were the men. Reitrin knew most of their names by week three. She started to greet them by name when she saw them. Whether or not they answered. She didn't smile at them though. She had a feeling a bright smile would not serve her well in her position.

It was the forth week of travel that Gechio had her call roll. She realized by this time she knew each man by name, and when she called their name she was able to make eye contact with them to make sure they knew she saw them.

She called the name Finn and saw a different man raise his hand.

"Caliber, put your hand down," Reitrin said when the man responded to the wrong name. "Finn, respond I call your name. You're not new to this."

Caliber and Finn had looked dumbfounded.

Reitrin had no issues with roll call after that.

Gechio had been snickering.

Their journey took more than two months to complete. When they came near their destination Hiro and Gechio brought Reitrin to the edge of a wooded cliff. It overlooked a long plot of land that was barren except for a large encampment surrounded by a tall fence with barbed wire curled over the top. There were lookout posts at every corner and armed guards everywhere.

"Some kind of holding camp," Reitrin muttered.

"Yes," said Gechio. "Your job is to bring the prisoners there."

"My job?" Reitrin stared at him.

"All the men here are low rank." Gechio nodded over his shoulder. "Farmers or young men recruited against their will, so you don't outrank them."

"We choose who will take over before we leave," Hiro explained. "We cannot rank you, but since you are no lower than the rest we can put you in charge."

"Why me?" Reitrin asked. "I know you want to protect me from the men, but I'm capable of protecting myself now."

"You're more level-headed than these guys," Gechio grumbled. "They're all brawn and no brains."

"That's a little harsh," Reitrin said. She looked

up at the black sky. Two months and the sky remained dark. Reitrin knew they were the same clouds as the ones in the Real World.

Aoiro had been right.

"Odd clouds," Reitrin said. "Do either of you know what's up with them?"

"Yes," said Gechio.

"Classified," Hiro added with a touch of warning.

"I know, I know," Gechio grumbled.

Reitrin stared at them. "Wait, you know what's going on?"

"Classified," Hiro said again.

"It's a bit of a secret," Gechio shrugged, grinning. "The clouds are following us, but when we leave they'll stay over that camp for a few more–"

Hiro stomped on Gechio's foot. "Classified."

Gechio rubbed his foot and cursed Hiro.

Reitrin's mind spun. They knew what was happening. The clouds were following them. They'd stay over the camp for how long?

What was going to happen?

"After handing off the prisoners, I suggest you take your men and run for your lives," Gechio whispered to Reitrin.

Hiro stared him down.

"Okay," said Reitrin.

Gechio left to check on the troops and Reitrin stood alone with Hiro.

She removed her hat, pushed back her bangs from her forehead and then replacing the hat. From here she would be expected to take charge of the men. There was a lot she didn't know and her heart raced with fear when she thought about it. What would she do if the men refused to listen to her?

Maybe abandon them and go find Etakai? Reitrin removed her hat again, raking her fingers through her hair.

"You'll be okay," Hiro told her. "Gechio and I made sure you were prepared. All you have to do is lead."

"I don't remember learning how to lead," Reitrin muttered.

"You watched us, copied us, and can preform as we have," Hiro explained. "You're ready. Trust me. Gechio and I are confident you can finish the last leg of the journey without us."

Reitrin bowed her head, but then looked sideways at Hiro. "What will happen to you and Gechio when you leave?"

"That's classified," said Hiro.

Reitrin sighed.

Hiro glanced at her, but then looked over his shoulder when Gechio approached them.

"We need to go," said Gechio. "The holding camp cannot see we were involved."

Hiro nodded once. "The men know to follow Ray?"

"Yes," replied Gechio. "We will properly turn them over to her before we depart." He looked at Reitrin who was fiddling with her sleeves. "Don't be nervous. You're the stern leader of these men now. If you look anything less than confident it'll reflect badly on Hiro and me."

"Sorry, sir," said Reitrin. "I'll make sure the men get to the camp as soon as possible."

"Better," said Gechio. "Just play the part until

you find your friend. Then you can get yourself out of this mess however you see fit. Go AWOL or something, they don't have real records of you so you'll be able to disappear with ease."

Reitrin smiled with gratitude, then followed as Gechio and Hiro led her back to the camp where the men were taking down tents and extinguishing fires.

When Gechio returned with Hiro and Reitrin the men fell in and stood waiting. Reitrin looked over them. Her stomach felt like it was rolling. The men were disgruntled already and gave her cold looks.

"Ray has been selected by Hiro and I to lead you to your destination from here," Gechio called to them.

Reitrin heaved a sigh. The weight of their glares was extreme.

"Your orders are to deliver the prisoners to the camp," Gechio explained. "New instructions will be given to you when you arrive. For now you're excused. Behave for Ray. If you do not we will hear about it."

Some of the men muttered and looked at Reitrin begrudgingly. She would meet their eye, holding their gaze until they looked away.

Gechio looked up at the clouds, then turned to Reitrin. "They're in your hands now."

"Will a female soldier be mistreated when we arrive?" Reitrin asked.

"You shouldn't be," Gechio said, rubbing his chin. "The man in charge of the camp is a little creepy though. Wouldn't you agree?" He looked at Hiro who shrugged.

"Come on." Gechio led them into the camp.

"Give the order for them to prepare to move out,"

Gechio hissed under his breath.

Reitrin's heart was racing. She was not sure if she would be okay.

"Everyone," She called, her voice echoing out. "Prepare to move out. You have ten minutes." She saw a few men give her sloppy salutes, but others just obeyed with scowls.

"This is not going to be fun," Reitrin sighed as they passed through the camp.

"Be a leader, but also be yourself," Gechio said as they exited the camp. "We have to go now. Take care of yourself. Remember, they don't have paperwork on you, but if your friend is alive they may have information on him at the camp."

"That's why you're sending me there?" Reitrin asked in surprise. She hadn't expected them to have an ulterior motive.

"You have to complete the mission since we got you here in attempt to save your life," said Gechio cleverly.

"And because he has a soft spot for women," Hiro muttered.

"Stop saying that," Gechio snapped.

Reitrin smiled sadly at the two of them. She had a feeling their story was much more complicated than she could ever guess.

"Take care, guys," she said.

"If anything goes wrong, just run away," said Gechio. "You can disappear, just keep us erasers a secret when you do."

Reitrin nodded once in reply.

Hiro stepped towards her and patted her on the head. "Shoot anyone that gets too close."

Reitrin laughed. "Of course."

The erasers left and Reitrin watched them until they disappeared into the forest.

Ten minutes were up.

Reitrin turned on her heel and strode back into the camp. She passed the cage of prisoners without glancing at them.

"Let's move out!" She called to the men. "Finn, James, go on ahead and find a safe route for the horses. We're heading down hill from here."

A few lazy salutes met her orders as she strode on. At this point she didn't expect nor care if the men followed her.

One more week and it will have been three months since she came to this storybook. With no sign of Etakai her hopes were falling and she set her hand over her abdominal. She had kept the belt dry for so long. Her wound no longer hurt. She was in great condition despite being a little hungry and sore.

All she needed was to find Etakai and they could go home.

Reitrin glanced back. Her heart jumped to see the company following her. She had expected them to let her run off alone.

Either way, it didn't matter. Like Gechio said, she could run away if she wanted to. But if the holding camp had answers about Etakai's location then she was determined to go there.

Finn and James returned from scouting ahead.

"There's a safe path ahead," said Finn. He was a young man, and rather quiet, but he had a prankster's spirit. His hair was brown and floppy, his eyes gray and energetic. He, like the other men, was skinny, but muscular from training.

"It looks like the path is used often," James added. He had brown hair, but his eyes were also brown and he was a little taller than Finn. "And there is mud too so we should proceed with caution."

"We'll have to keep an eye open for others as well as move slow," Reitrin muttered as she walked with them. "Good job. Please help with the prisoners cart. They may get antsy now that we're near our destination."

The two nodded once and left her.

Reitrin moved on, able to hear the company at her heels. It was reassuring to hear the men following her, but she wondered for how long they would stick around.

The hill leading down to the level ground was still slick. Reitrin had the men help stabilize the horses and the cart. It was slow going. The mud made it worse than it should have been. Reitrin kept close to the company, but did not offer her help. To do that now would be seen as getting in their way. She kept a sharp eye on them and the path ahead as they gradually made their way down.

When they reached flat ground Reitrin felt like she could breathe again.

She led the company across the empty field at the foot of the hill. When they approached the camp they walked along the fence. It was made of barbed wire and thick metal poles. Behind the fence there was a long distance of space before the first row of barracks appeared. They looked bigger up-close than they had from the hill. Reitrin gazed at them, but then peered down a long opening they passed. She saw no signs of life among the buildings. Nothing moved, but she heard shouting coming from deep within the camp.

It took them nearly two hours to cover the distance of the camp and finally round to the front. The men on watch called out their approach.

Reitrin and her men were greeted by a group of soldiers dressed in cleaner clothing than theirs with freshly shaved heads. These men had not weathered the same trials Reitrin and her soldiers had.

"Good job, men," said the leader of the camp. He was a general and wore a fine uniform that fit his air of pride. He saluted, clicking his heels, and Reitrin copied. "I am General Schevia and I oversee this camp. We were pleased to hear the skirmish ended in our favor." He stared at Reitrin as if he had only then realized she was female.

"Not a captain or man of commanding rank?" The general whispered to himself, looking over the ground before him. "You all have done well to come here safely."

"We brought prisoners," said Reitrin, making Schevia look at her. He seemed annoyed to have a woman speak to him. "Can your men handle them?"

"They can indeed," replied the general. He snapped his fingers and several of his men shouldered their weapons and hurried to the cart to take the hostages into the camp. "I can see you men have not eaten a proper meal in a long time." He eyed the grumpy soldiers standing at attention behind Reitrin. "We will have a meal prepared for you."

"We appreciate it, General," replied Reitrin.

Schevia scowled for a moment. "Why do you speak for the men?" He asked this in a less-than-friendly tone.

"I was left in charge," Reitrin replied. She hoped he couldn't see her trembling beneath the weight of his glare. Gechio and Hiro had not prepared her to be addressed by other soldiers. She was just a woman here. Historically speaking she could have been killed for acting as a soldier. Was this book historically correct in that aspect?

"Were you?" The general looked intimidating. He looked past her to the men. "Can you confirm this?"

"Sadly," said Johnson. "She was deemed more level-headed and so put in charge."

"By all of you?" The general asked.

Reitrin heart sank. They weren't supposed to speak of Hiro or Gechio. As far as they were concerned it was supposed to be just them on the journey.

. "Well," said James, moving to stand beside Reitrin. "She is rather scary."

Reitrin stared at him.

"And what man would complain about watching a lady walking ahead of them?" Caliber chuckled.

Finn elbowed him in the ribs.

"Are those the barracks for your men?" Reitrin glanced past Schevia, noting a small gathering of makeshift houses collected outside the fence.

"Yes," replied the General, following her gaze. He was quiet for a moment, but then a scowl came to his face. "You can be given a separate room, given you're…" He looked down at her sourly without finishing his sentence.

"I'd appreciate that." Reitrin made a mental note

to get her questions answered as soon as possible and escape this place. She didn't like the general. He was giving her goosebumps.

To add to her unease, the General faced her and said, "You may dine with me in my quarters, if you don't want the company of these stinky men."

Reitrin decide this man was a complete creep. She was surprise when she saw James go rigid at his words.

"I'd rather stay with my regiment," replied Reitrin.

"Then I will see to it that a separate room is prepared for you," said the General. "But you are still welcome to dine with me if you desire."

"I'll appreciate the room, sir," said Reitrin, trying to make certain he knew she was not interested in his dinner date.

She looked up when his soldiers passed, leading the prisoners in a line. Reitrin watched Charles who did not look back at her.

"Will we be partaking of the duties of the camp until our orders arrive?" James asked this, drawing the general's attention.

"I will send word to HQ that your regiment arrived safely," the General answered. "Tonight you can eat and rest without worry."

Reitrin gazed at the camp. She felt cold when she saw how lonely the place looked. There was also a foul scent drifting through the air that she could not describe. The black clouds above them made matters no better and Reitrin looked up.

"We should adjourn to shelter," said Reitrin. "It could start raining again at any moment.

"Agreed," replied the general. "If you and your men may follow me, I will bring us to the mess hall where your regiment can be refreshed." He turned and walked away, leading the group of weary soldiers.

As they walked, three of the men came to Reitrin's sides.

"What a creep," said Johnson under his breath. "We may all be starved dogs out here, but that doesn't mean he can snatch you up without a fight."

Reitrin set her hand over her mouth to stop from laughing. "None of you will be snatching me up. I'm out here looking for my fiance."

"So you're saying we should stick with you until we find out about his fate?" James raised an eyebrow with a clever grin. "Til death do you part."

Johnson hit him over the head.

Reitrin chuckled. "Thanks, but there's no need. He's alive. I just have to find him."

"We could help you search," said Finn, pushing James aside. "Please?"

Reitrin rolled her eyes. "Don't start acting like you want to be friends."

"Hey, Johnny, you called her scary," Finn told Johnson. "Do you really think that?"

"Don't you?" Johnson replied. He lowered his voice. "Anyone who can befriend erasers is scary in my book."

Reitrin shushed him with an uneasy look at the general. If he had overheard, he didn't show it. Reitrin gave Johnson a warning look. "We never met them."

Johnson shrugged, but didn't argue.

Ahead of them was the mess hall. It was a long house that was wider than the barracks lined up near it. The company climbed the stairs into the warm cafeteria. The tables were being washed by women in gray clothes.

The general left them to ask the cook to warm some stew for the guests. He then returned and directed Reitrin to a table disconnected from the rest. Reitrin pretended to ignore him and sat with her men instead as they filled two tables and chattered back and forth.

Reitrin looked down the table at the men. She hadn't realized she had grown used to them. Seeing them smiling and teasing each other made her grin.

Until the general dropped into the seat beside her.

"Where can we find the records of your enlistment?" He asked.

Reitrin clenched her jaw. "I don't know where such documents would have been kept. I was recruited as a civilian against my will."

"Women are rarely enlisted."

Reitrin had expected this. The story line bent that law. In the real civil war women were not permitted to fight. Her circumstances were not normal though.

"I don't know what to tell you, sir," said Reitrin as food was brought to them. "I strayed too close to the battle ground while searching for my fiancé."

She loved how the word made curious men draw back a little. But like the others, the general leaned in once again.

"Any luck finding him?" Schevia was just like the others. A woman can't be engaged to a dead man.

"He's alive," Reitrin retorted. "I just have to find

him. Do you have any men here that go by the name Etakai?"

"Our prisoners are given a number," Schevia replied. "Like cows for slaughter, you don't want to give them a name or risk getting attached."

Reitrin held her breath, staring at the table with wide eyes. No, that wasn't how it was supposed to be. The camps were only meant to hold prisoners of war and keep them safe. Right? What kind of nightmare had the writer of the book created? Was Schevia one of the characters in the book?

Reitrin found herself wishing she had read the book before she entered it.

"Where did you take the prisoners we brought?" Reitrin asked. Her voice shook and she cursed herself for it.

"The most recently built barrack," replied the General. "We continue to gain more prisoners than we can hold. Our process of clearing them out is messy and so we build more barracks in hope of sparing lives."

Reitrin's gaze was hollow. Their process for cleaning them out? What was he talking about?

Running away was starting to sound good.

"Could I speak to them?" Reitrin asked, meeting the general's eye.

"I see no reason why you should."

Reitrin looked away, but then glanced down the table at the others. They were being served soup and chattering back and forth happily. Reitrin looked down as a bowl and spoon were placed before her with a glass of water.

"Eat up," said the general as he left. "I have

things I must tend to."

He left and Reitrin stared after him.

"He's a dog," Finn hissed to Johnson. "I bet he's gunna give her his personal room."

"I hope not," Reitrin grumbled. She was starved from travel, but she couldn't bring herself to eat. If she could find no answers here then she needed to leave.

"Maybe we should go into the camp and find him?" Johnson suggested to Reitrin. "The general doesn't want you to have hope of finding a rival for him, but I bet the prisoners would tell you if they knew the name."

"It's possible," said Reitrin. "Can we enter the camp? Wouldn't it be dangerous?"

"Of course," said Caliber. "Especially for you. Step out of sight and you'll get–"

Johnson hit him over the head.

Reitrin knew what Caliber had been about to say. "If we can get in, I would like to. This is the last hope I have. If I can't find anything here..." She faded to silence and shook her head. She would have no more ideas. Etakai would basically be lost to her. How could she find him in this huge world?

The men finished eating and Reitrin left with a few of them behind her.

They went to the gate and the soldiers on guard let them inside.

"It's getting late, don't take too long," one of the guards warned.

"Understood," said Reitrin.

The guard gave her an icy look when he realized she was female. Reitrin wondered if she stopped speaking if anyone would realize she was female.

Why did that annoy her?

She fought the urge to look down at herself to see why her figure wasn't a good enough hint as to what her gender was. Maybe men in the book were just dim? Reitrin decided to go with that.

Walking through the camp was eerie. The prisoners that were on break sat in group glaring at them. The men that were working ignored them.

Reitrin stayed close to Johnson and Finn.

They drew near the workers that were building new barracks and Reitrin gazed at two men sitting on the roof. They were familiar, but from such a distance she wasn't sure why.

Reitrin wanted to go see them, but just then there came shouting from behind them.

Schevia was coming. He marched up to them in a rage with papers in his hands.

"Your regiment," he said, showing Reitrin and the others the papers. "Did you come in contact with erasers?"

"Huh?" Reitrin's heart dropped. Gechio said no one was supposed to know about them. How did Schevia?

"You mean Hiro and Gechio?" Johnson asked.

"We know of them," Caliber shrugged. "Ditched us with this girl in charge."

Reitrin as staring at Schevia with a pale face.

"You, your regiment, and your prisoners are to be questioned and then killed," said Schevia. "The erasers are a classified military secret. Anyone unauthorized who know of them must be put to death."

The men were alarmed and Reitrin's stomach clenched.

This was not how things were supposed to go.

Chapter Twenty-One
Not Close Enough

Etakai could have kicked himself for not realizing it sooner. The black clouds had moved in slowly, bringing a storm with them. Now they lingered, on and on, and he knew they were the same ones in the Real World. More than once Etakai paused in his work to look at them. Their presence made him uneasy.

It was a few hours into the work day when he heard the disturbance. There was no way of knowing what was happening, but he heard people shouting about new-comers. He had no time to look around since he was perched on an unstable roof with nails and a hammer. Not only that but he had recently received another beating

He hit his thumb with the hammer.

Cursing, Etakai looked up when the clouds broke and rain began to fall. He heard Shilo calling him by his number and Etakai looked around. There were soldiers, but they had brought strangers who were wearing the clothing of the rest of the prisoners. One of the men was strikingly familiar, despite his recently shaved head Etakai's heart leapt. He climbed down the ladder.

"They will be added to your barrack," the soldier was saying. He cast Etakai a dark look as he spoke. "Make sure they know how the job is done." At that they shoved the new prisoners towards the barrack and left. The soldiers on guard returned to their posts.

Etakai walked forward, smirking at the man who returned the look.

"I'm glad you're alive," said Etakai, offering Charles his hand. "I could have sworn you died."

"The same to you," replied Charles, shaking Etakai's hand. "Why didn't you tell me you have a fiancé?"

Etakai gave him a blank look. "Because I don't. Where did that come from? You hit your head too hard?"

"Nah, a woman was looking for you–"

The guards barked at them to get to work and Etakai, sensing another beating, had no choice but to climb back to the roof in the rain. Charles took the pail of nails from Shilo and climbed up to help.

"She was cute," Charles said as he handed Etakai a few nails.

"I don't know any women from around here," Etakai said as he hammered in another board. There was a stack of lumber beside him that he had to use up before the day was done.

"So how did she know your name?"

Etakai shook his head. "It's suspicious." He had a bad feeling, but he wasn't about to tell Charles about it. Charles knew nothing of the storybook worlds. If Etakai told him what he was thinking Charles would assume he had lost his mind.

Etakai suspected someone from a storybook had come looking for him to finish him off.

He hit his thumb again and cursed angrily.

"You'll need to wrap that up," said Charles as Etakai's thumb began to bleed. "In a place like this a small infection could kill you."

"I know," muttered Etakai as he wrapped his thumb in his shirt and pressed on it until the bleeding stopped.

"So are you curious?" Charles asked.

"About what?"

"Your wannabe fiancé."

"Not interested," growled Etakai. He continued working. Laying down long boards and hammering them in place.

Charles handed him nails and watched the other men working. In the rain it was uncomfortable, but not as uncomfortable as sitting in a cage for over two months.

A commotion came from the front of the camp. Charles turned to watch, but Etakai ignored it. He was used to such things happening. A fight between prisoners, or a dispute between guards. None of it was uncommon.

"Oh hey, speak of the devil," said Charles. "Its your wannabe fiancé."

Etakai looked over his shoulder. Several men in shabby uniforms were walking through the camp. Some men in nicer attire were with them. It looked like they were fighting.

"She should keep the hell away from me," Etakai growled, going back to work. It had to have been an assassin sent by Fevros or Aoiro. He had been in the book for months. How much time had passed in the Real World?

"Oy!" Called a guard.

Etakai and Charles looked down. One of their guards was waving him down.

"I think I'm in trouble," laughed Charles. He left

the pail of nails with Etakai who glanced at him.

"Be careful," he warned.

"I can tell they're ruthless guards," Charles grinned. "You're a mess, did you know that? I'm sure I'll be back." He saluted and climbed down the ladder.

Etakai's bad feeling grew worse. He watched Charles as he was led away, but then Etakai saw the shabby soldiers were also being taken away.

What had just happened? It was likely they weren't allowed inside the camp. But why wouldn't they welcome new guards?

"None of my business." Etakai turned back to his work. He had fallen behind in his work load because of the appearance of Charles and his injured thumb, the last thing he wanted were more distractions. He finished the work before the trumpet sounded. When he and Shilo climbed back down Charles was still gone.

Etakai glanced around and hoped Charles would be okay. He joined the others and headed back to the barrack.

That night he could not shut his eyes. Shilo was curled up against him, fast asleep. The other men were also sleeping despite the roll of thunder over their heads. Etakai lifted his eyes to the ceiling, but just then the door was thrown open at the same time the thunder banged above their heads.

"Up!" the soldiers roared as they marched in. They pulled people to their feet and shoving them aside.

It was a walk-out.

Etakai knew he would be taken. He could see the

first soldier making a beeline toward him. When Shilo jumped up to protect him Etakai was quick to pull him back and stand up instead.

"You're called Etakai, right?" The soldier asked.

Etakai's eyes widened. How had they learned his name? They were only called out by number.

"How do you–?"

He couldn't finish when the man seized him and shoved him to the exit.

Etakai saw the others staring at him in horror. This was what they had dreaded. The day the man who wanted to save them was taken away. Etakai cursed himself for not realizing this would happen so soon.

Was it the fault of the wannabe fiancé? Had she pulled some threads to get him killed? That was what Etakai got for refusing Fevros's offer this long. If he didn't call out to Fevros he would die.

And so Etakai determined to die. He would never call to Fevros for help.

Etakai was marched across the dark ground through the pounding rain. He could hear nothing but the sloshing footsteps and angry raindrops drumming the roofs and ground. The soldiers had taken no other prisoners. Etakai was the only one in the group who had no idea where they were going.

They were taking him to the front of the camp. He found it strange that there was a large group of shabby shoulders waiting for them.

As they came closer Etakai realized the shabby soldiers were bound and gagged. He wanted to stop, but a gun stabbing him in the side forced him forward.

"Please, stop this," a woman screamed. It was the wannabe fiancé. Had she planned all of this to make Etakai cave? A damsel in distress, innocent men about to be slaughtered. It was the kind of sick scheme Fevros would plot to make him cave.

"I cannot go against my orders," Schevia told the woman. "According to your men you were with the erasers the most. You will be questioned and then killed."

"No!" The woman kicked and struggled. She was crying now.

Etakai glanced towards the woman as she was dragged away. It was pitiful to watch. Was she really an enemy? Etakai wanted to save her. She had a familiar voice that sent shivers up his spine.

Fevros was playing a cruel game. He had somehow made the woman's voice sound like Reitrin's. He would have fallen for it if he hadn't known Reitrin died in the Real World.

Etakai was struck across the face and shoved to the ground.

"To the fence," said the general. "I want her fiancé to die too. There's no telling what he may know."

"Is the other man done being questioned?" One of the soldiers asked the general as Etakai was dragged to the fence. "Isn't he to be brought out here with the rest?"

"He's done being questioned," Schevia answered. "But no, he won't be joining us out here. His dead body will help loosen the girl's tongue when she arrives."

Etakai overheard these words and searched the

faces of the men on either side of him.

His heart sank.

Charles wasn't with them.

"No." Etakai lifted his head, staring at the ring of armed soldiers before him. Etakai's heart began to race.

His dying body … no. They couldn't be talking about Charles, could they? Where were the other prisoners? Etakai looked around again. Had they been killed? Why was it these men weren't supposed to make it out of the skirmish alive?

What were the erasers?

"Ready weapons," the general called.

The line of guards shouldered their weapons, then lifted them to ready position.

"Take aim."

Etakai blinked the rain from his eyes and watched the firing squad. The barrels of fifteen rifles aimed at them. Etakai heaved a sigh, his breath coming out as mist. He wished he could have done at least one heroic thing before this day came.

"Wait a minute." Etakai laughed. "Oh, this place sure did a number on me. I forgot who I am again."

The men on either side of him glanced at him.

"Ready," the general called. "Fire!"

The guns rattled and the bullets thudded, but not into the prisoner's bodies. The firing squad lowered their guns at once and the general stared speechlessly.

A long blue shield stood between them and the prisoners. The bullets were lying spent in the mud.

Etakai stood up, facing them with his blue eye glowing.

"I think I've behaved for long enough," Etakai

said in a cold voice. He pulled down the cloth that hid his green eye and strode forward. "I won't play nice anymore." His green eye flared to life.

"Fire at will," the general shouted.

The guns went off and the bound men threw themselves into the mud to avoid the onslaught. Etakai lifted his hand, the blue light blazed around him, protecting him and the men behind him. He did not have his knives, but that didn't matter.

When the guns fell silent at the same time the men hurried to reload. They hadn't been prepared for a fight. Etakai laughed.

He ran forward. His fist collided with the jaw of the closest soldier, knocking him senseless. In the same motion Etakai spun and kicked the next soldier in the back of the head, making him lurch forward. Etakai whipped around and slammed his knee into his face.

Etakai was too close to shoot. The soldiers swung their rifles at him or tried to spar him, but Etakai weaved around their strikes as if he were water.

The soldiers were beat left and right and a few guns went off when they hit the ground. It was chaos and the general couldn't see what was happening. He saw a flash of blue light here and there, and it was always followed by a scream of pain.

Schevia had never seen anything like it and instead of fighting he turned tail and ran.

His boots splashed in the mud and he almost fell on his face twice. He shouted for the men at the gate to let him out and they hastened to obey.

Once outside the camp the general ran to the general's barracks.

Only one room had lights on and he raced inside. He threw open the door.

There were four soldiers, a dead prisoner in the corner, and tied to a chair with a dark bruise forming around her right eye was Reitrin.

"You," said Reitrin as she gave the general a dark look. Her lip was bleeding and she looked ready to pass out. "I ought to shoot you. Hiro would love that."

"Silence!" shot the general. "Anyone who saw the erasers has to die."

"Then should you die too?" Reitrin lifted her head and glared at him. "You knew they were going to be there. What kind of screwed up story line has an entire regiment of soldiers killed for a secret like Hiro and Gechio–?"

Schevia struck her across the face. "I told you to be silent."

Reitrin lifted her head and spat blood at the general's feet.

The soldier on her left struck her face for it.

"I need more men sent into the camp," said the general. "Some kind of demon is attacking us."

"Demon?" Reitrin's eyes widened and she looked up. "Do his eyes glow like fire?"

Schevia glared at her. "You knew all along what he was, but you failed to warn us."

Reitrin snorted, but this made her wince. "I'm glad I didn't. I hope he kills you all. If he's seriously ticked off you don't have a prayer."

Schevia's lip twitched.

"Leave her to die with him," he barked to his soldiers. "Whoever kills the demon earns a years worth of pay." He and the soldiers left.

It wasn't quiet. Reitrin heard gun shots and shouting from the camp. She blinked blood from her eye. It was drizzling down her forehead from a cut. Her body was aching and her sigh blurred, but she couldn't pass out. Etakai was near.

"Don't … go far away, Etakai," she whispered, trying to wriggle her wrists free from her binds. "Don't go … where I can't find you." She grimaced and felt tears prickling in her eyes. She was so close. He was outside. She just needed to reach him and they could go home.

Her struggling made her chair toppled over and she hit the ground. She yelped. Her arm was throbbing from her weight in the chair landing on it. Reitrin cursed, but then heard movement behind her.

"Hold still, miss," whispered Charles.

Reitrin's heart jumped. "I thought they killed you." She couldn't turn her head far enough to look at him. "They shot you."

Even so, the man dragged himself towards her. Blood was dribbling from the hole in his chest and spilled from his lips, but still he managed to seized the ropes binding her wrists.

"Don't move so much," gasped Reitrin. "You'll kill yourself."

"I'm already dead," whispered Charles, his weak fingers fumbling with the knot of her ropes. "I died when my men fell in battle. It was nice to see Etakai still alive. he's the last one alive from our regiment now that Schevia killed the rest of us."

Reitrin gritted her teeth. "Hiro would be furious if he knew what was happening. Charles, I'm so sorry. You'd be fine if I hadn't come here."

The sounds of the fight rang out in the night. It was only drowned out by momentary bursts of thunder. Reitrin could hardly think straight and when she felt the ropes binding her loosened.

She struggled to pull her arm out from under the chair and untied her ankles. She shoved the chair aside and collapsed beside Charles. She rolled him onto his back and stared at him.

"Charles," she whispered. "Hang on."

Charles laughed weakly. "You're … odd. You aren't … from this world, are you? It's like you're–"

He cut off, coughing up blood and pressing his hand to the bleeding wound in his chest. His breath was rattling in the wound and Reitrin's stomach rolled.

"Thank you," she whispered to him. "Thank you so much. For everything."

Charles smiled. "Happy to help … Take care of Etakai."

"I will," Reitrin replied. "I will."

Charles said no more. His last breath left, long and deep, and then he was gone.

Reitrin sat in silence beside him. His blood coated her fingers, but she didn't wipe it off. She lifted her head, the tears racing down her face as she listened to the battle outside.

"Etakai," she whispered. "I'm going to give you such a scolding when I find you." She looked over her shoulder, but then rose to her feet.

It was time to find him and go home.

Reitrin stumbled out of the barracks, her arms and legs bruised from the soldiers pummeling her.

She hated them, but there was no need for revenge. This world was just a story.

Outside the rain was blowing back and forth and whipped her short hair around. She blinked through the darkness and saw the shadows of men fighting each other. Some had guns and others were being overpowered. It looked as if the entire camp was fighting. There was no sign of blue or green light.

Where was Etakai?

Reitrin hurried to the camp, knowing she would likely be struck down by a stray bullet. She didn't care. Etakai was close.

She was almost to the fence when a group of men came running out to meet her. Reitrin fell back, prepared to fight them off if she needed to.

"Ray!" It was Johnson and the rest.

Reitrin's heart leapt. "You're okay?" She ran to them. The shabby men were the most familiar sight in the story. "You're all okay?" She stumbled and Johnson caught her.

"We were saved by the demon," said Johnson, helping her to stand.

"Where is he?" Reitrin tried to run past him to the camp, but Johnson stopped her.

"It's a mess back there, we need to leave."

Reitrin froze. "No," she whispered. "Wait, no!" She tried to fight out of his grip, but he was too strong.

"It's not safe," Johnson yelled, trying to hold her back. "You'll be shot before you find him."

"We can't leave!" Reitrin was hysteric as she struggled and fought to get to the camp. Finn helped Johnson grab her and they pulled her away from the camp. Fear tore through her heart. She was too weak to stop them from taking her away.

Etakai was slipping from her grasp all over again. "Not again."

They were leaving. The camp faded into the distance. Reitrin was in tears. No. He was there. She was so close.

"Etakai!" She screamed.

The thunder and wind drowned out her voice.

Chapter Twenty-Two
The Hollow Victory

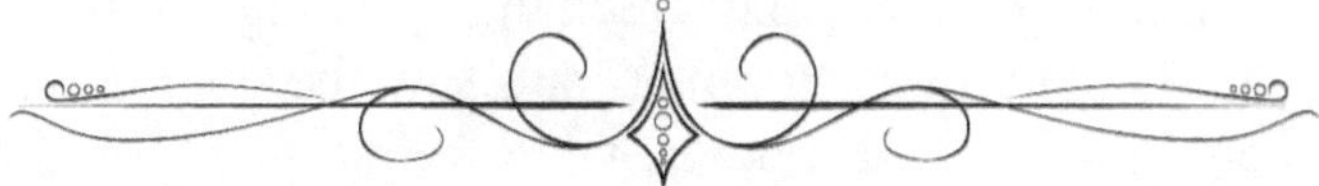

As soon as the scruffy soldiers were freed Etakai ran to the barracks, shouting for the men to wake up and fight. His voice was rough by the time he finally reached his own barrack. The guards on patrol were running into the camp as the prisoners burst out of their barracks and met them. Some overpowered the guards and took their guns while others were shot down as soon as the doors opened.

Etakai threw open the door of his barrack.

And froze.

Everyone was dead. Each one had been shot and killed. The barrack reeked of blood and Etakai picked his way through them. He realized they must have been killed after he was taken away. As he searched he knew what he would find, but it made the discovery no less painful.

Shilo.

It looked as if the others had tried to protect him since there were five men piled in front of his body. Etakai dropped to his knees. His expression was hollow and his hands were limp. There were no words and no reason. Etakai sat there and listened to the fight going on outside. He was enraged that his comrades, the men who had respected him, had been murdered in their beds.

Etakai shot to his feet. His green eye was burning and he strode to the door. He burst outside, but before he could cause havoc one of the prisoners ran to him.

"We've taken the camp, Captain!" He shouted, holding up a rifle.

Etakai blinked, the green light fading from his eye. He stared past the man and saw the guards had been killed. Their bodies were being piled in the middle of the camp and the gates had been busted off their hinges.

"We have sent men to gather our belongings from the soldier's encampment," the man explained. "Do you wish to join them?"

Etakai was still in a daze. The fight was over so fast. He sharply shook his head. "Yes." He forced himself to shake off his rage and strode out into the rain.

The man fell into step beside him and offered the rifle, but Etakai ignored it. All he was after were the knives the soldiers had taken from him. He felt defenseless without the throwing knives strapped around his waist.

Walking through camp he saw the prisoners pointing at him and talking about him. It was as if they had all known about him, which he had hoped for. Now they seemed to fear and admire him. Their faces were not friendly, but they showed no signs of hatred.

Etakai crossed the camp. At the gate he found the last surviving guards were kneeling with their hands on their heads and the prisoners in a ring around them.

"Captain," said one of the prisoners, a young man with rage burning in his eyes. "What should we do with them?"

Etakai stopped in front of the guards and looked

down at them. They stared at his dark glare with pale faces. One was the guard who had enjoyed beating Etakai without reason. They looked pathetic kneeling before him unarmed and frightened. Etakai scoffed and strode past them.

"Do as you like," he said without looking back.

A few men laughed and the guards cried out for him to have mercy, but Etakai closed his ears to them. He saw Shilo and the rest of his men's dead bodies when the guards spoke.

The makeshift houses were being prepped to burn. The prisoners were stealing all that was good and laughing as they found items that had been taken.

"Captain, are these your knives?" A scrawny man with a tangled beard asked this. He showed Etakai the belt of throwing knives.

"Yes, thank you," he said, taking the belt. He lifted his shirt, strapping them on and then left to search the other houses. The first one he came to was filled with the stench of blood and as he stepped inside he saw the toppled chair, the ropes, and the familiar man lying in a pool of blood.

Etakai stood in the doorway, his jaw clenched. He walked forward, looking down at Charles's empty eyes. There was also a smell of the familiar blood that was haunting him. It smelled of Reitrin and he recalled the moment she was stabbed, then the empty eyes of Shilo came to his mind, and now he looked down at Charles's lifeless body.

Etakai placed his hand over his eyes and began to laugh. He laughed hard and some of the men came to check on him. They watched him with worry as he laughed out loud with his hands over his face.

"Captain?" A man whispered.

"Without fail!" Etakai laughed. From beneath his hands there were tears rolling down his face. "Without fail, if they befriend me they die. Every damn time!" He dropped to his knees and slammed his fist straight through the hardwood floor. The men jumped and one ran away.

Etakai reached out and shut Charles's eyes, his tears tapping the face of the man he had called friend.

"What are we living for?" Etakai whispered to Charles as he knelt beside him. "Why do we fight?" Etakai shut his eyes and bowed his head. After a moment of silence, he rose to his feet and heaved a deep sigh.

"Burn the buildings down," he said, turning and facing the men. "We need to find safety, but the camp won't offer that. It won't be long before they send more soldiers to kill us."

"Captain," whispered one of the men as Etakai left the house and joined them outside. "Are you sure? These buildings are warmer than the barracks. We could stay here until–"

"We won't be staying here," Etakai interrupted, looking over his shoulder. "We will need to disappear into the forest. They know we're here and we've killed many of their men. They won't rest until we're dead, so we need to flee." He headed to the camp and the men followed him.

"What of those who don't want to come?" they asked.

"Let them leave," replied Etakai.

"Are you sure we're in danger?"

Etakai stopped in his tracks and rounded on

them. "How many of us have already died? If we're not in danger then this world has a funny way of showing it. Don't you agree?"

Chapter Twenty-Three
Fated Friends

It was three days before Reitrin finally washed her hair. Her men had found an abandoned house far from the camp only a few days ago. Reitrin had been too crestfallen to care what happened so they had to lead her the entire way. To them it was only logical that the woman was upset. After all, she had been close to finding her fiancé, only to be forced away from him for her own safety.

Failing to reach him left Reitrin feeling hollow and lost. She shut herself in the room, staring at the ceiling trying to figure out what she could do next, but she kept giving up and trying not to cry from the overwhelming exhaustion and disappointment.

Etakai could have been miles away from her again and she didn't know where to begin searching.

Johnson brought her meals and Finn took turns with Caliber guarding her door. There were sixteen soldiers staying in the house, and for some reason they seemed determined to stick with her.

As Reitrin washed her hair in the sink she pondered why they would want to protect her. She had put their lives in danger. They should have abandoned her by now.

She sighed and dried her hair. There were clean clothes lying beside the bowl of cold water she had been using to wash. The water was brown from dirt when she finished and she left her towel beside it. She changed into the jeans and blue sweater the men had found for her. All of them had changed into civilian clothing and burned their uniforms.

The house they had found was well-stocked. It had been evacuated due to the camp nearby, but the family that lived there would have planned to return, so all their belongings were still inside.

The days they spent in the house was the coziest for Reitrin and the men. They had good food, running water, and soft beds, but Reitrin had avoided the others for too long because of her depression. She decided it was time to rejoin the group.

Reitrin dried her hair more as she looked in the dusty mirror at her reflection. Her short hair was uneven and the bruise around her eye had faded. She still had a cut on her lip and her skin was pale now that she had washed the dirt and blood off. Reitrin frowned at her reflection. She did not look like the girl that had first entered the history book. She wondered if Etakai would look different too before she left the room.

She could hear the men chatting down stairs. The house was a large Victorian mansion with white walls and golden-yellow details. It was richly decorated beneath the dust. Reitrin felt like royalty as she walked down the spiral staircase to the next flight of stairs that led to the ground floor. She crossed the large entrance hall, glancing nervously out the giant window to the black clouds that had not left the sky. She watched them for a moment, but then went into the next room.

The men looked up at her.

"Ray," said Caliber, leaping to his feet. The rest of the men copied.

"You're out of your room," said Finn in surprise, hurrying to her side. "I leave my post for a minute and you actually come out?"

"Way to go," said Johnson, coming up behind Finn and knocking him over the head.

Finn scowled and Johnson grinned at Reitrin. "How are you feeling, Ray?"

"I'm okay," said Reitrin gently. "But I feel like I've wasted a lot of time. I'm sorry I was sulking for so long." She looked over the faces of her men and managed a smile. They looked healthy and content. She was pleased, but then her gaze wandered to the window and she wondered again about Etakai. "I wish I had found him."

"It wasn't safe for us to linger," said Johnson with regret. "I would apologize, but I see no reason to. Any one of us could have been struck by a stray bullet back there."

"I understand," said Reitrin. Her gaze kept going to the window. Soon the men were looking outside too.

"Those clouds freak me out," said Thomas, a blond man whose beard was growing in thick. "I could swear they showed up after that skirmish months ago."

Reitrin narrowed her eyes. "They did, didn't they."

"I've never seen anything like this before," said another man named Jake. He stood and went to the window, leaning on the sill and gazing outside. He carried a rifle with him at all times. "It feels like the end of the world."

"It can't be," said Reitrin.

The men looked at her as she folded her arms.

"I've seen this before," she said. "And you know what? I think I want to find out what's causing it. These clouds won't go away until we find out why they're even here. Gechio mentioned that he and Hiro had something to do with the clouds."

"Well, that can only mean one thing," said Johnson. "A visit to the lab."

Reitrin blinked and looked at Johnson. "Lab?"

"Gechio said it's supposed to be a secret," Johnson explained. "But since we were with them Gechio accidentally spoke of it. He may get in trouble for this, but it's the only lead we've got."

"And finding it will be the next problem," Finn sighed. "Can't we just stay here?"

"We can only live comfortably for a little while," Reitrin told him. "Eventually the owners of this house will return. Besides, it's an adventure. Do you want to be bored forever?"

Jake shrugged, but then laughed. "Not at all. I just didn't trust those guys. They fought like demons in the battle."

"Kind of like that guy with the glowing blue eye," said Johnson quietly.

"That man is my fiancé," muttered Reitrin.

"What?" half of them demanded.

"Etakai," said Reitrin sadly. "I lost him before I joined your regiment. I managed to track him to the holding camp. Then, when I was close to finally finding him, I was dragged here." Her voice shook and she coughed to clear it. She remembered then that she needed to remain strong in front of the men. They were acting nice, but that didn't mean she was completely safe. She had pushed her limits being depressed for three days, now she had to regain their respect, not earn their pity.

"I'm sorry," said Johnson. "It wasn't safe."

"No, it's fine," said Reitrin as she forced a smile. "Do we have anything to eat? I'm starving."

"Yeah, come on," said Finn, leading her to the kitchen.

Reitrin followed, but she wasn't sure what to do now. She wasn't hungry, she had just wanted to change the subject.

When she reached the kitchen she realized most of her men had followed her. She looked back at them with surprise. Johnson was at the front and his hand shot to his head, rubbing his shaved scalp sheepishly.

"We just wanted to know what you planned on doing next."

"Oh." Reitrin gazed at the men, but then went to the table in the middle of the kitchen and sat down.

Finn was fetching the leftovers of recently made sandwiches and stew the others had eaten for lunch.

As she waited, Reitrin contemplated how to answer Johnson's question. She tapped her nails on the table and sighed. "I need a map."

Jake left the kitchen at once to find one.

"The lab won't be on a map if you wanted to find it," said Johnson as he and the others joined her around the table.

"No, so that's why we'll head to whatever place is farthest from civilization," replied Reitrin. "A place tucked away where civilians wouldn't wander. That is where we will find the lab."

"What about finding your partner?" Caliber

asked.

Reitrin scowled. Finn placed a bowl of stew and a sandwich in front of her and she watched it.

"Well, at this point I can't be sure he's alive. That massacre could have been the end of him." Not likely, she added in the back of her mind. She knew Etakai was a fighter and wouldn't let anything stop him from surviving. There was a hope he would also look into the black clouds.

"So we focus on the clouds?" Johnson asked.

"Yes." Reitrin took a bite of the sandwich and was grateful for it right away. She ate more, feeling her energy returning and her mind clearing.

Jake returned with a map and rolled it out for her. He used bowls and cups to keep the corners down and Reitrin moved her food aside. The map was old. The house where they resided had a circle around it.

"Looks like there's a town beyond these trees," said Finn, leaning close over Reitrin's shoulder. She cast him a cold look and Finn sidled away at once.

"There are quite a few blank spots," muttered Caliber. "How do we know which one to check?"

"One with the most cover," suggested Johnson.

Reitrin examined the map carefully as she sipped stew and smacked her lips. She nodded a few times and then tapped an empty space in the middle of the map.

"The camp was here. And we are here." She pointed at the circle. "We traveled about this far to get to the front of the camp when we first arrived." She traced another line along the trees and field. "So this is where we parted with the erasers. From this point Hiro and Gechio went this way," she slid her finger along the map to the end and tapped a large gorge that was unmarked.

"We've avoided that land," said Jake.

"The erasers kept us away," murmured Johnson. "Now that I think about it, cutting through there would have shortened our journey."

"Sounds like they're hiding something there," said Reitrin, finishing her stew and sandwich.

"If we get all the way there and find nothing we risk being caught and killed," Finn murmured.

"We're civilians now, remember?" Reitrin said, brushing crumbs off her sweater and leaning forward to examine the map more. "We're in danger either way, but civilians may hold a better chance of survival. The general wanted us dead so it's safe to assume others will as well. I say we find this lab. There's nothing wrong with posing as normal people."

"Normal people carrying rifles and pistols," Johnson laughed.

"Plenty normal at wartime," replied Reitrin.

"So should we pack up and get ready to leave?" Jake asked.

"Let's relax a little longer," said Reitrin, heaving a sigh. She tapped her spoon to her chin and frowned. "I'm rather annoyed right now. I hadn't realized so much would go wrong in the camp, and it all happened so fast too that I couldn't think of a counter measure."

"If you delaying our departure gets us caught will that make you feel better?" Caliber asked none too gently.

Reitrin raised her eyebrows at him.

Johnson stood up. "Don't speak to her like that."

"No, he's right," Reitrin interjected. "We don't want to risk sitting around here any longer. This house will be one of the first places searched so we should pack up and leave." She pushed back her chair and stood. The men around the table stood with her. "Get ready. We leave in an hour."

The men loaded up backpacks with supplies and extra ammo for their firearms. When they finished they met Reitrin outside. She was standing with the map folded and a compass in her hands. She was checking their best choice of direction, but her expression was grim.

"Do you need help?" Johnson asked as he came to her side.

"No," replied Reitrin distantly. "I was just thinking." She looked off into the distance, but then at Johnson. "Is everyone ready?"

"We are," replied Johnson, looking back at the men. Each of them carried a backpack with supplies. "Are you?" Johnson handed Reitrin her backpack, which she glanced at before taking and flinging over her shoulder.

"Yes, let's move," said Reitrin, slipping her other arm through the second strap. She began walking and the men followed her. It was silent as they went. Their weapons clacked and some of the men held onto them to hush the noise. The ground was still soft so they left footprints. Reitrin took note of this ruefully. It would not be hard for enemies to track them.

It was slow going, but Reitrin knew she was in no rush. Aoiro told her he had found a brief mention of the black clouds in the book. This was what she was supposed to find. This was the other goal he said she may manage to accomplish.

They walked until the sky began to darken more. In the shadows they saw distant outlines of what had once been the makeshift houses. They had been burned to the ground and the fence of the camp had been torn up as well as if someone had been scavenging the barbed wire. Reitrin resisted the urge to check it out.

They were under the cover of trees when the rain began to fall. Reitrin ordered them to stop and they made a temporary shelter by stringing branches together. There was no reason to risk starting a fire. Reitrin checked the map again, but something didn't feel right. They were in the forest near the camp, but that wasn't the thing unsettling her. She searched the trees, wondering if this was what it felt like to have someone watching her.

It was as if a hand was on her heart, telling her she was in the sight of someone that could be potentially hazardous.

"We're being watched," Reitrin muttered, checking her compass.

Her men had already been silent before, but now the silence grew tense. Reitrin folded the map and slid it into her backpack. "Johnson, go with Caliber and check it out. Be extra careful. We weren't the only ones that escaped that camp."

Johnson shouldered his rifle with a nod. He and Caliber stood and headed into the woods. Jake, who was on watch a ways away, glanced at them, but then looked away. The other men were watchful too.

"How would she know we're being watched?" Caliber whispered as he carried his rifle under his arm.

"She's different," muttered Johnson. "I'm sure you and the other men have noticed it also."

Caliber nodded. "A great difference between her and other women. Quiet, assertive, and even a little scary. No wonder the erasers liked her."

"I don't know where she came from," muttered Johnson, slowing to a stop as they came upon a small brook. "But I would almost venture to say she's not from our world."

"That's far fetched," said Caliber, but he didn't question it. He and the rest had seen the glowing blue power of Reitrin's fiancé. They knew he was a demon and they wondered if she was anything like him. Were they both monsters?

"I can't see a thing," said Caliber, searching the woods. "If there's someone out there they probably left already."

"No, I'm still here," said a cold voice from behind.

Johnson and Caliber whipped around, but they were both seized and slammed to the ground. Their arms were pinned by the men who had been hidden nearby and their rifles were removed. The two men struggled, but they stopped when they saw the blue glow.

"You," said Johnson in surprise. "You're the one that saved us from the firing squad."

The demon stepped into their sight, his shaved head had signs of silver hair growing and his body was wrapped in bandages. He looked eerie and his different colored eyes were hollow.

"You were the shabby soldiers," muttered the demon, sinking to one knee between them and looking from one to the other. "Why are you coming this way? There is nothing to be found in these woods except us."

"We're looking for the lab where the erasers live," Caliber blurted out.

"Good job, loose lips," grumbled Johnson.

The demon sat back on his heels with his eyes narrowed. "Why? Are you going to ask their help to wipe out the soldiers that betrayed you?"

"Nothing of that nature," Johnson said. "Our leader thinks they may know why there are black clouds in the sky."

The demon arched an eyebrow, but then looked at his men who watched him with puzzled faces. "I am curious as to why your leader would wish to get to the bottom of the black clouds." He turned his attention back to Johnson and Caliber. "Not one of my men thought there was an issue. They were determined to wait for the clouds to fade."

"We were the same way, but our leader said she had seen them before," said Caliber quickly. "Please, don't kill us."

The demon smirked. "Kill you? The thought hadn't crossed my mind."

Johnson and Caliber were puzzled.

"We're keeping tabs on you," explained the demon. "But you were armed so we had to detain you. Most everyone who meets me wishes to kill me."

"You saved us so we wouldn't have thought of

it," Johnson replied.

"Who is your leader?"

"Her name is Ray."

"And she's seen the clouds before?" The demon's gaze appeared to pass through the ground between them. He was silent for so long that even his men looked uneasy.

"Captain Etakai," whispered one who was holding down Johnson.

Etakai's head snapped up, but then he leapt to his feet.

The men looked up at once as well when they heard the click of several guns.

"Release them," said Reitrin, aiming at Etakai.

Etakai turned around and stared at her. He blinked, but then motioned for his men to release the prisoners. Johnson and Caliber collected their guns and hurried past Reitrin, standing behind her. She was glaring at Etakai.

"Look at you," Reitrin snapped. "I have been searching for you for months until I lost track of the days, but I kept searching. Do you have any idea what I've gone through to find you, Etakai?"

The men with Etakai looked puzzled, but Reitrin's men moved back. This was now a personal vendetta.

Etakai was motionless. He faced the barrel of Reitrin's gun without batting an eye. His face was pale though. "You died. You couldn't have survived that wound."

"So you ditch all of us?" Reitrin replied curtly. She lowered her gun. "You idiot! Did you hope to accomplish something by running away and deserting me again?”

“No,” Etakai retorted.

“So then why did you leave?” Reitrin demanded. “Why did you abandon me again?”

Etakai winced at her words. “Abandon you? I was doing everything in my power to save you!”

“And you did,” Reitrin shouted. “I’m standing right here because of you. But why did you leave?”

“I was scared!” Etakai yelled. “I’m not used to fear and I don’t know how to deal with it. I was tricked into coming here. I’ve had a lot of time to think about things and I swore if you were alive I’d never leave you again!”

Reitrin recoiled and Etakai glared at the ground.

Neither he nor Reitrin cared that their men were uncomfortable.

“You would have needed an Eysheus to bring you here,” Etakai said in a calmer tone.

“He couldn’t,” Reitrin replied. “He sent me after you. I owe you, Etakai. And now I owe him too for helping me get here to find you.”

Etakai could hardly find words. “All this time … I thought you were dead.”

“But I’m not.”

Etakai nodded then bowed his head. “I’m sorry.”

Reitrin sighed. “I never thought I’d live to see you of all people acting humble.”

Etakai stared at her for a painfully long time. When he finally moved it was to approach Reitrin.

Reitrin’s men lifted their rifles, but Reitrin held up her hand for them to remain at ease. She set her rifle down and stepped forward to meet Etakai.

They stood facing each other and Etakai stared at

her with disbelief. It seemed like he couldn't breathe as he lifted his hand and carefully touched her face. His hands were rough from work and dirt, but there was warmth. His fingers were trembling also and he sharply took his hand away.

"I thought you were dead," he whispered hoarsely. His emotions finally broke loose and tears burst from his eyes. He crashed to his knees and Reitrin was shocked when he wrapped his arms around her legs and cried into her knees.

The men on both sides felt awkward, but they had no idea that Reitrin was in the same boat.

"Come on, it isn't that bad, Etakai," said Reitrin, managing a smile, but it wavered. She was fighting back tears. "I'm alive, and so are you. Now we can find out what's with the black clouds and go home."

Etakai was shaking his head, but whenever he tried to speak all that came out were failed attempts. Reitrin sighed and pushed him back. When he looked up at her she knelt in front of him and wrapped her arms around his head, holding him close.

"I hope you know I only put my life in danger for friends," she told him gently. "Whether you like it or not, Etakai, we're friends now."

Etakai tightly shut his eyes and held her tight. "I'm sorry … I'm sorry." It was all he could say.

Chapter Twenty-Four
The Crystal Crier

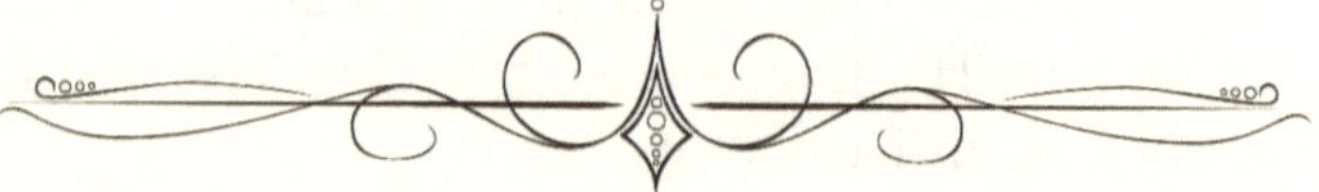

The two groups made camp, setting up tents and lighting fires for warmth. They chatted with one another like old friends, even though they were supposed to be enemies. The topic they brought up most was the chaos at the camp and how the guards had almost killed their own just because of Ray. They would look towards her and Etakai whenever her name came up. She and Etakai were seated beside a fire and Reitrin was helping Etakai clean his injuries.

"The house we found had a lot of helpful stuff," Reitrin said as she dabbed the dirt and blood off a festering welt on Etakai's shoulder. "I'm glad we brought a lot of the medical supplies with us. You're injuries are awful."

Etakai did not speak as she cleaned the wounds. He had been beaten often in camp and it seemed to Reitrin that he had never taken time to care for the injuries. There were cuts and bruises all over his body, but the wounds he had received from his time in the other storybooks had healed. The long scar across his back from the giant scorpion was white and gnarled.

As Reitrin cleared the blood smears off his skin Etakai glanced at her face. He watched her, but she didn't notice. He frowned.

"You're hair doesn't look nice that short."

Reitrin gave him a cool glare. "It's not my fault. A machine cut it for me."

Etakai looked confused, but Reitrin didn't feel like explaining that Hiro had cut her hair.

"Why did you leave the hospital like that?" Reitrin whispered this question as she put aside the blood-drenched rag and fetched a new one. "I know we don't get along, but you are supposed to be a hero, aren't you? What kind of hero runs away like that?"

Etakai sighed. "I told you, I was scared. Fear wasn't something I experienced in my book. Not like that at least."

"I'm sorry you had to learn it in the Real World."

Etakai was quiet for a moment, but then bowed his head. "People who become my friend always die or betray me. I thought you were dead, and it was my fault." He looked at Reitrin who met his gaze. He looked away with shame.

Reitrin blinked. Witnessing Etakai opening up to her was giving her mixed feelings. "How long have you harbored an interest in the Real World's history?" She asked this question to change the subject. She hadn't expected Etakai to wince and look away.

"I don't. Fevros fooled me."

"Fevros?" Reitrin raised her eyebrows. "Isn't he an Eysheus?"

Etakai nodded. "I discovered too late that he is evil." He told her of the portal that took him to the library and his discussion with the Eysheus.

Reitrin listened with a scowl as he told her how Fevros wanted him to become one of his servants.

"I was supposed to fall so far I would call him to save me and in return for his help," Etakai ended in a weary voice. "To become his loyal dog."

"You're a hero this time," Reitrin told him.

Etakai looked back at her bitterly. "Don't butter me up. I abandoned you in the hospital. I know I'm not a hero."

"Being abandoned is something I'm getting used to," said Reitrin, setting aside another rag. She took a jar of salve from her bag and opened it, collecting some onto her fingers. "My mother died and as a child I thought she had abandoned me. My father and sister acted like it was my fault too, so even though they were there I was alone. Then you ditched me twice. It's turning into a common occurrence." She sighed and smeared the salve over his bruises.

She was unaware of Etakai's sturdy gaze locked on her face.

"I never had friends," Reitrin told him. "I avoid people because I know if they learned that my family blamed me for my mother's death they'd leave. No one wants to be friends with someone accused of murder."

"But you're friends with me," Etakai told her. "We both know I've killed people. So you shouldn't be friends with me."

"If you ever say that again I won't come save you next time you need me," Reitrin said, clapping the jar shut and returning it to her bag.

"You haven't saved me," said Etakai bluntly.

"Haven't I?" Reitrin wondered. "It seems to me like you were stuck in this story until someone could get you out."

"And do you have a way out?"

Reitrin held his gaze for a moment, but then looked away. "I'm not sure."

Etakai sighed and the conversation ended.

Reitrin began to bandage his wounds. As she worked she couldn't help but notice how many pale scars covered Etakai's body. She found herself wondering about his story and the battles he had fought.

One scar in particular was along his collar bone and appeared to have been a stab straight into his chest from above. Reitrin tried not to stare, but just then Johnson ran up to them.

"Guys!"

"What?" Etakai and Reitrin asked in unison. They gave each other sharp glares and Johnson looked uncomfortable being the one to cause the glaring.

"Something is coming," said Johnson to them both. "We had men watching the sky from the tree tops, but one of them spotted something on the horizon."

"What did it look like?" Reitrin asked as she rose to her feet.

"You may not believe me," said Johnson. "But it looked like a person in black armor."

"Douse the fires!" Reitrin shouted. "Take cover!"

At once the fires were put out all around and the men sought shelter finding in the darkness of the trees. Reitrin left her fire glowing.

Etakai looked up at her.

He was surprised despite his best attempts not to be. He had never thought Reitrin could become the person he now saw.

There was a buzzing in the air and Reitrin retrieved her rifle from the ground. She shouldered it and watched the treetops.

BANG!

Something made of steel slammed into the ground before her. Dirt flew in all directions.

The stranger slowly straightened up. All around him where black wisps of cloud from the sky. It swirled around the man that was indeed a person in armor. The armor was black with silver edges and looked sharp. It was layered like spikes and there was a winding sound that came from it whenever the person moved. The sound was familiar and Reitrin stepped forward, placing herself between Etakai and the eraser.

"Hiro."

The machine lifted its head. Its black hair was slicked back and there was a black visor clapped shut over his eyes. A mask covered its nose and mouth, but it slid open, revealing thin lips that had red lines drawn from the corners of his mouth to his chin.

"Ray," whispered the clear voice. The visor snapped open and Hiro's golden eyes looked at her. There were tears rolling down his face. Red lines crossed his face from the corners of his eyes, making him look like a machine. "You are the rebel force I was sent to eliminate."

"Eliminate?" Reitrin asked. "Why?"

"There is never a why," replied Hiro. "There is only succeeding to eliminate."

"But you helped me," said Reitrin quickly. "Why would you eliminate me now?"

"My orders are clear."

"You were nothing like this in the other story." Reitrin saw Hiro's eyes widen.

"Hirochi?" Etakai stood up, examining the

machine. "Why is he here?" He looked at Reitrin who met his gaze.

"I think this is his story," she answered. "He might be a part of the Real World's history."

Etakai stared. "That can't be possible."

Hiro lifted his head, listening to them, but then glared. "My orders are clear."

"Fine, kill me then," said Reitrin, moving forward and holding out her arms.

"Idiot," Etakai hissed.

"Keep out of this," said Reitrin without breaking eye contact with Hiro. "If you would be so kind, before you kill me, could you tell me everything you know about the black clouds? Dead men tell no tales, right? And I desperately want to know what they are before I die." She eyed the wisps of black cloud dancing around him. It reminded her of something.

Swarms of bugs.

Hiro's blinked slowly as if processing her request. "I told you it is classified. Why would you request this again before your death?"

"In my world these clouds come back," replied Reitrin. "The only thing similar between now and the future is your presence."

Hiro straightened up, but then his armor sank into his skin and faded. The sight turned Reitrin's stomach. Beneath the armor, Hiro wore plain black clothes.

From around him the clouds faded, but Hiro reached out and grabbed at them. "I could be dismantled for not killing you right away. He looked at Reitrin with his fist closed. "I have little time before they send someone to find me and ask why you're not dead. I believe what you have told me, and so I will tell you."

Hiro approached Reitrin. He was aware of Etakai's defensive stance, as well as the watchful soldiers in the trees. Hiro opened his hand and Reitrin saw in his palm hundreds of small black dots.

"I have heard them referred to as micro bots," Hiro told her. "These in my hand can absorb moisture in the air, created fabricated forms of weather, and block out the sunlight. My creator has a machine that can made trillions of these in a day. They are her greatest work. Each one has a drop of nitroglycerin inside them."

"What?" Reitrin's heart sank. "But that–"

"Will cause an explosion," Hiro confirmed. "They fill the sky, creating unmovable black clouds. Their program has them under orders to avoid contact with anything. They cannot be caught. Except by me." He looked at the micro bots in his palm. "They seem to like me. Perhaps because they think I am one of them, since my programming is similar."

"What do you mean similar?" Reitrin whispered.

"We were made to cause utter destruction," Hiro replied. "I can wipe out an entire army, and with enough of these bots gathered, they can wipe out entire cities."

Reitrin looked back at Etakai who held her gaze.

"Castroph City," Reitrin could hardly breath. She swung around to look at Hiro. "Can we stop them?"

"They are drawn to a devise," Hiro explained. "Gechio carried it on our journey earlier. He left it in the woods, so the micro bots remain near the camp." He glanced at the sky. "Ah, I'm running out of time.

If you find the devise and destroy it the bots will no longer receive the signal to swarm and will safely return to their lab. If the timer on the devise reached zero the bots will fall from the sky and explode."

Reitrin was alarmed.

"Their numbers determine the magnitude of the blast. That means the more there are, the more disastrous the event will be. I have witnessed the experiments–" He was cut off when someone slammed into him.

"Get to work, Crystal Crier!" The man who spoke wore a cloak stained dark with blood. The hood and coil of the cloak hid his face, but Reitrin had recognized the voice.

"Gechio."

Gechio looked at her, but before he could speak Hiro tackled him and the two rolled away. Reitrin saw the hidden soldiers jump out of the way. Above them the sky was darkening. From the sky there came a sound like distant rain rattling on a steel roof.

"It's happening," said Etakai as if impressed the machine had told the truth.

"We need to get away," said Johnson, running to Reitrin. Behind him the other men were racing to escape the two erasers that were bursting apart trees as they fought.

"No," Reitrin rounded on Johnson. "I have to see what will happen."

"We'll die!"

"None of us can run fast enough to escape the sky falling." Johnson watched the darkness falling towards them.

"Captain!" One of Etakai's men shouted. They

were looking at the sky. It was so dark only the faint embers of the fire pits could be seen. They heard Hiro and Gechio fighting, but the sound was drown out by the crashing of millions of small micro bots descending upon them.

"Reitrin, we should leave," Etakai whispered, wrapping his arm around her shoulder so they wouldn't be separated.

"Not yet," said Reitrin, watching the sky. "I want to see what will happen."

"We may not have time to escape by then," Etakai said. "And you said you don't know how to get us back."

"I don't care," said Reitrin. She grabbed his wrist, waiting and watching with bated breath.

The bots struck the trees. Above them the explosion went off. The ground rumbled and the fire fell towards them.

Reitrin screamed. It was too fast. She clung to Etakai and with all her strength willed them from the pages of the book as trees burst into pieces and flung branches and fire around.

The explosion stopped.

Silence filled her ears.

It was a deep silence, but there was a gentle thudding in her ear. Reitrin heard the heartbeat, but then became aware of the arms around her. She felt the warmth of the person she clung to and her face blushed when she remembered the only person it could be.

She lifted her head and blinked a few times to clear her vision. Her eyes focused on Etakai who held her gaze.

He seemed relieved and sighed with a smile. "That was horrifying."

"Yeah," said Reitrin. She looked around. They were in her bedroom inside the apartment. By their feet lay the book. Reitrin looked down at it. "And it'll happen again if we don't destroy the devise. I wonder if Hiro knows where it is?"

"How did this happen?" Etakai asked.

"I asked Sia and Shan to keep the book in a safe place for when we returned–"

"Not that. You took us out of the book."

Reitrin stared up at him as the realization dawned on her. She was a human from the Real World, she shouldn't have been able to book jump at all.

"You … you're right. What does that mean? I'm not an Eysheus. I'm from the Real World."

"I don't know." Etakai looked pensive. "We may need to look into this."

The door flew open and the light turned on.

Etakai and Reitrin looked up to find Sia and Shan staring at them.

Sia's face turned red and Shan recoiled in surprise.

"How long have we been gone?" Reitrin asked.

Sia shrugged and then broke into a fit of giggles. "I don't know, but do you two need more time?"

"What?" Reitrin looked at Etakai who met her gaze with a puzzled face. They were still holding each other and, on top of that, Etakai was shirtless.

"Oh!" Reitrin exclaimed as she shoved him away. "No! Not at all."

"We could use some answers though," said Etakai, pretending nothing embarrassing had just occurred. "How long have we been gone?"

"A few hours," replied Shan. "Etakai, what happened to you guys? You both look awful."

"We were in a war," replied Reitrin grimly. She realized she still wore a pistol at her hip. And then she remembered all that Hiro had told her.

"Ah!" She rounded on Etakai. "Why are we standing around? We have to find Hiro and the device before the city is destroyed!"

"What are you talking about?" Sia demanded when Reitrin shoved past her and Shan.

"We have no time to explain," Reitrin yelled.

"Wait! What about your injury?" Sia cried. "What happened?" Sia looked at Etakai who stood up and casually walked past them to follow Reitrin who was fumbling with the deadbolt.

"The micro bots blocking out the sky could fall at any minute," said Etakai. He took Reitrin's shoulder, stopping her frantic attempt to unlock the door with her trembling fingers. "You'll never get anywhere being this frantic."

"We have to hurry though," Reitrin shot.

Etakai unlocked the door. "We're in this together. You running around like a crazy person won't help the situation."

"But we don't even know where Hiro is."

"Of course we do," said Etakai cleverly. "Chief of the Secret Police. You and I came to the conclusion he was Hiro when we met him. It has to be him behind those sunglasses."

"Then we need to get in contact with him."

Etakai grinned. "And I can do that. Just watch."

Chapter Twenty-Five
The Black Clouds

Reitrin and Etakai left the apartment and stood on the snowy sidewalk. Etakai lifted his hand and his green eye glowed. He shot an orb of green energy into the air and it exploded above them.

Reitrin had watched this and gave Etakai a blunt look. "That's it?"

"Of course," replied Etakai. "The Secret Police will sense my energy and come. Oh, wait a minute." He crossed his arms and frowned. "I didn't think this through,"

"What do you mean?"

"Well, I could draw more to us than just Hiro this way. Other enemies know my energy, and now they know my location too."

Reitrin slapped her hand to her forehead.

There came a sound of guns clicking and Reitrin looked at the top of the apartment.

There were five men in bulletproof body armor standing on the roof, armed and waiting. Only one of the men did not wear a helmet.

"Hiro!" Reitrin called, waving to him. "We need your help!"

The Chief straightened up, but then nodded to the men with him and the five of them leapt of the building and landed in a circle around Reitrin and Etakai.

One of the men stumbled and ruined their graceful entrance. A man with long black hair smacked his helmet and cursed at him.

Hiro walked up to Reitrin and Etakai, slipping off his glasses and watching them with contempt.

"Never yell my name on these streets." His golden eyes had a soft glow of warmth behind them. It was surely Hiro, but there was something completely different about him. Neither the Hiro working with Aoiro, nor the eraser, had looked as alive and capable of emotions. "How do you know my identity?"

"I suspected you since I met you outside Shan's old restaurant," Reitrin replied. "Etakai and I were just in a historical fiction novel and we met your younger self."

Hiro scowled at this.

"He had a lot less emotion than you," Etakai said.

"I have had a long and hard life." Hiro heaved a sigh and folded his sunglasses, hanging them from the front of his body armor. "I have been expecting my cover to be blown for some time now. I just hope you don't spread word that the Crystal Crier is still in the city. I had a bad reputation here."

"We won't," said Reitrin. "But we do need your help. We know about the device and you have to help us find it. You're the special police, right? You should be dying to help us."

"Secret Police, Ms. Nichol," corrected Hiro bitterly. "You have a funny way of asking for help."

"Will you help us?" Etakai asked. "If you won't we have to get going. Finding the device is our priority right now."

Hiro shook his head, but then looked at the men around him. "Spread out and keep watch. I'll try not to take too long."

The men saluted and then ran off in different directions.

"The device was made when I was still new to my destructive powers." Hiro turned back to Etakai and Reitrin. "I have been hunting for the device these past few days when I recognized the micro bots gathering. I cannot locate it though. It is small, rectangular, and white with a green light that blinks red when it was about to expire."

"When it expires the bots blow up?" Etakai asked.

Hiro nodded. "It can be activated by hand, or set to a timer. I'm not sure how much my former self could have told you, but I'm certain the devise is on a timer."

"Can we trust your memories?" Etakai asked. "You're a little old. Is there a chance you're thinking of some other device?"

Hiro was still for a moment, but then he gave Etakai a rueful glare. "I'm as sure as I was back then. I'm not like you humans. My memories do not fade. I can recollect anything from any moment of my life perfectly if I wish. Thankfully, I can also store bad memories in the back of my mind where I will not stumble upon them by accident."

"That sounds like a nice feature," said Reitrin with a sad smile. "I wish I could do that."

"Back to the matter at hand," Hiro cut in before anyone could start reminiscing bad memories. "The problem with history books, fiction or non, is that an Eysheus can return to it time and time again and find it the exact same way. It is not like fictional storybooks that can be changed. History is cement. An Eysheus could go into your story and bring back a feather and because of that the story could get messed up and dissolve. In a history book, if something is removed, as soon as the Eysheus leaves it is replaced as if nothing had ever happened. The device can be found again and again as long as the Eysheus knows where to look."

"How do you know so much about Eysheus?" Etakai asked suspiciously.

"I have been the Golden Protector for some time now," Hiro answered. "In my time working to keep the book jumpers secret from the Real World I have learned many things. Don't push me, boy."

"Could the device be in another city?" Reitrin asked. "Sia said the black clouds go on for forever."

"The device covers a long distance, but it is not unending. The Eysheus must have taken every last micro bot created to cast this great a cloud in the sky. I'm unsure why the devise has not been activated yet. I can't guess what the Eysheus is plotting."

"More handsome men?" Sia appeared behind Reitrin who jumped. She hadn't noticed Shan and Sia join them.

"The Eysheus who took it enjoys games," Hiro told Reitrin, ignoring Sia's comment. "My men and I have tried to think as he would, but our attempts to find the devise are not enough."

"So … we need to think like an Eysheus?" Reitrin asked thoughtfully.

"Yes."

"Have you thoughtfully searched the library then? And any surrounding book stores?"

"We have."

"How about the roof?" Reitrin looked down the street in the direction of the library.

Hiro followed her gaze. For a moment he was quiet, but then he shook his head. "We did not think he would place it out in the open so we did not check the roof."

"I will if you won't," said Reitrin.

"Okay." Hiro swept her into his arms and shot into the air.

Reitrin screamed in alarm and grabbed Hiro's jacket. She heard the whirling of gears inside his body as he passed through the darkness. Hiro landed on a nearby building as light as a feather.

"Wait, what about the others?" Reitrin gasped, shaking uncontrollably. It had all happened so fast she was dizzy.

"I don't enjoy wasting time," replied Hiro as he ran to the edge of the building and shot into the air again. Reitrin was sure she had left her stomach behind.

They landed on the library's tower and the two looked up to the top of the decorative steel point aimed at the sky.

"Look," Reitrin gasped as Hiro set her down and steadied her. It was still snowy on the angled roof of the library. "A green light."

At the top of the point there was a faint green glow, so small it could have been mistaken for the reflection of a creature's eye.

Hiro carefully went to the tower and climbed to the top. He was still for a moment as he looked at the familiar device.

"She was right." He shook his head. "Figures. I was looking in all the wrong places." He plucked the device from the library and slid back down to stand beside Reitrin who gazed at the device.

It was exactly as Hiro had described.

"It's not on a timer," Hiro muttered. "Odd. Why would it be left manual? Did they plan to leave the cloud above Castroph forever?"

"What do we do now?" Reitrin asked.

Hiro crushed the device in his hand. The machine beeped, but then the light went out. "We do that." He held up the machine that dangled with wires and a smashed hard drive. "Now we see if it worked. There's a chance this was a decoy."

They looked up at the black clouds and waited.

For a while it seemed nothing had changed, but then a soft rattle like leaves blown by the wind filled the air. The black clouds began to shift and they thinned.

It felt like they watched the sky forever. But then stars began to appear. A warm breeze passed through the city and the snow started melting. The sound of the bots faded to nothing and Reitrin held her hand over her mouth.

"It's clear," she whispered. She slipped on the icy tower, but Hiro caught her arm.

"I'll have to have my men track the micro bots and find out where they land," said Hiro to himself. He knew Reitrin wasn't listening. Her eyes were sparkling as she gazed at the sky.

It felt as if the sky had been dark for centuries. A crescent moon hung in the sky, glowing gently.

"We did it," Reitrin laughed. "I can't believe we

actually did it."

"It was too easy, young lady," said Hiro, his eyes scanning the city.

His words made Reitrin's joy vanish. She stared at him. His golden eyes were full of suspicion.

"There's no way someone would let a weapon as powerful as this be discovered so easily and conveniently." He looked down at Reitrin who seemed insulted by his comment about it being too easy. "Ask yourself this, what else could have been going on while we were occupied with this?"

Reitrin frowned at him. "You think it was a distraction?"

"The clouds caused a lot of panic," Hiro murmured. "Any chance to discover how to get rid of them would be our main objective, as it was. Then when we found it there was no timer, so it's possible they had no intention of destroying the city. It would have been a perfect time to cause chaos without us noticing–"

An explosion across the city made them look up.

Reitrin's heart dropped. "I think that was near my apartment."

Hiro threw aside the crushed device, grabbed Reitrin, and shot off towards the commotion.

Chapter Twenty-Six
Green Fire

Etakai wasn't sure why he had a bad feeling again. Hiro had practically kidnapped Reitrin before their eyes, but that wasn't the only thing that bothered him. Something was making him uneasy.

His time in the history book was still fresh in his mind so he was tense and he felt vulnerable. He wore his throwing knives, but for the first time in his life he wished he was carrying a gun. In his storybook he would have been prepared, but now there were factors he couldn't balance. Different stories called for different forms of defense. He had been lucky to survive as long as he had, but even though he hated to admit it he knew he couldn't turn a blind eye to his weakness.

He was only a storybook character, but that didn't mean he couldn't attempt to be more.

"Who was that?" Sia asked, making Etakai flinch at her annoying voice. "Was he another storybook character?"

"No," said Etakai. "He's as real as you."

"What?" Sia stared at Shan who shrugged.

"Anything is possible," he said. He looked ill and kept rubbing his arms. It was cold still, but then warmth fell over them.

They all looked up to see the black clouds fade and the clear night sky looked down at them.

Etakai's jaw dropped. "They did it?"

"Oh drat," said a voice behind them. "I was

hoping to watch you guys run around like scared mice a little longer."

A chill raced up Etakai's spine and he turned to look at the man standing down the sidewalk from them.

His blue eyes were clever, his fur coat pulled on despite the warm air, and his black hair was slicked back nicely. The twisted smile on his face made Etakai's heart clench.

"Fevros," he gasped.

Fevros chuckled. From his coat he withdrew his pipe and struck a match to light it. "Well now." He shook out the match and flicked it away. "I felt you return from history and I wanted to ask why you never called me."

"Because, I refuse to help you," Etakai shot, turning to face Fevros who set the pipe to his lips with a smirk.

"Etakai," Shan whispered. "Who is that?"

"His name is Fevros," replied Etakai without looking back. "He's an Eysheus who has been a pain in my side, making me do his dirty work, and then sent me into that history book where I was nearly killed."

"I wouldn't have let them kill you," said Fevros. He blew a smoke ring and watched it float away.

"I was almost killed multiple times!" Etakai spat.

"I'm glad you had a pleasant vacation." Fevros bit down on his pipe and grinned evilly. "Did you learn anything?"

"Not to trust you," replied Etakai.

"It would appear you didn't pass your test after all." Fevros sighed, blowing smoke thought his nostrils. "I'm disappointed. You were supposed to be mine."

"You're disgusting," Etakai growled.

"You don't know how long all of this has been going on," said Fevros. "You think black clouds and some misadventures mean it just started. I feel bad for you. What is it like to be so ignorant?"

Etakai took a threatening step forward, but Fevros was unaffected.

"You'll still be useful to me," he said. "But not for a while. You're too weak."

"I'm not weak," said Etakai darkly. "Here, let me show you."

He hurled three knives at Fevros, but the man sidestepped and swept his free hand up through the air, catching the blades as they passed him. He turned back, holding them out for Etakai to see.

"You can't hurt someone who knows your moves," Fevros said as Etakai stared at the knives in horror.

No one had caught his knives before.

"You take good care of these," said Fevros, biting down on his pipe so he could use both hands to examine the knives. "How nice." His blue eyes glinted and then Etakai found his own knives flying back at him.

All three thudded into his chest.

Etakai's eyes were wide. He felt his body crash backwards onto the concrete. The ache in his chest suffocated him, and the pain overcame him, filling his body and his head. He couldn't breathe. His sight was red from pain and starting to darken. The starlight looked strangely bright to him. When he tried to cry out his mouth was dry and blood filled his throat.

Was he dying?

Etakai clenched his jaw, but his sight was swimming. When Fevros stood over him Etakai couldn't focus on him.

"Pathetic." Fevros knelt on Etakai's stomach and prodded the knives. Etakai tried to scream, but only blood came from his lips. Yet it didn't taste like blood. The smell wasn't metallic, nor was the taste salty. It was something else, something stronger that made his eyes water.

"Awe, how sad," said Fevros when Etakai turned his head and spat the strange blood from his mouth. "You've never been attacked by me before, have you? Didn't you know if I cut you you'll bleed ink? After all, you're just a storybook character." He wiped the blood from Etakai's face, his fingers cold as ice. He held up his hand, showing Etakai the black ink smeared on his fingertips. "You're only ink and words, Etakai. Never forget that." Fevros stood up and Etakai struggled to rise.

Fevros tilted his head, but then leaned over him and wrenched the knives out of Etakai's chest.

Etakai's scream echoed through the city.

"I don't want you to survive this," said Fevros, dropping the knives by Etakai's head.

"Hey!" barked a voice.

Fevros glanced back casually at Shan who was shaking as he stepped forward.

"No one hurts Etakai and gets away with it in the Real World," Shan shouted, pointing at Fevros. Behind him, Sia was covering her mouth and staring at the scene with horror. "You won't get away with this!"

"What a nuisance," sighed Fevros. He lifted his hand and snapped his fingers.

The street exploded in a burst of light blue fire. The front of the apartment crumbled apart. Rubble was thrown everywhere along with Shan, Sia, and Etakai.

Shan crumpled to the ground and Sia crashed onto the street, holding her arms over her head.

Etakai tumbled across the pavement like a rag doll.

"You want to play?" Fevros laughed though the flames. He strode through the falling rubble, holding out his hand to sway the blue fire from touching him. "Your play mate is about to wake up. Good luck." He snapped his fingers again and vanished in a burst of light.

As soon as he vanished the flames turned from blue to orange.

Shan straightened up and beat the flames out of his hair. He looked around for the enemy Fevros had mentioned, but there was no one nearby. The smoke made him cough and he hurried to Etakai who was lying in the midst of the flames.

"You can't die now, Etakai," Shan pleaded. He coughed in the smoke. "We need you." He took Etakai by the shoulders to wake him.

Etakai seized his arms and kicked him straight into the air, then flipped backwards and landed on his feet.

Shan crashed to the ground, wheezing out when he lost his breath. He pushed himself up to his elbows and blinked through the heat of the flames to watch

Etakai who stood as if he were a marionette hanging from wires.

"Wh… what are… you doing?" Shan whispered. He could hardly breathe.

Etakai turned his head. His green eye was blazing like fire and his expression was empty. He lifted his hand and the green flames snaked down his arm before shooting at Shan.

Shan heard Sia scream. He was sure this was the end, but then someone seized him and threw him out of the way.

The green flames blew open the pavement.

"Get a hold of yourself!" The man who had saved Shan shouted.

Shan looked up to see a man with long black hair tied back. He wore the body armor of the Secret Police. A sword hung on his left hip and he had a pistol strapped to the other.

"Who… you?" Shan panted.

"I am Xitou," the man replied. "And I was brought here to help the Secret Police." He looked down at Shan.

Shan recoiled when he saw the long gash across Xitou's eye.

Xitou ignored Shan's stare and turned to face Etakai. He dove out of the way when more green flames flew at him like rockets. He drew his sword and ran at Etakai who hurled more green flames at him.

"Stop this!" Xitou yelled at him, knocking one of the fireballs away with his sword. "Aren't you supposed to be a hero?"

Etakai didn't respond. He lifted both his hands

and the flames snaked around his hands, shooting a torrent of flames.

Xitou flung himself behind a large chunk of rubble and cursed under his breath. The green flames smashed into the stone and flew over his head like ocean spray. Xitou flinched.

He looked past the rubble to Etakai who was watching where he hid. The green flames were mingling with the normal fire and they collected around Etakai. As he stood there, the normal flames turned green all around him and Xitou held his breath.

Etakai's eyes were empty as if he were dead.

"This is not good," said Xitou. "This is so not good." He heard fast steps and whipped around when someone leapt over his hiding place and rush Etakai.

"Chief!" Xitou cried when he saw the familiar man kick Etakai in the stomach.

Etakai crashed to the ground and Hiro raced behind the cover with Xitou.

"Are you okay?" Hiro asked. His golden eyes burned with rage.

"Barely," Xitou answered swiftly. "I saw Fevros show up and Etakai wanted to fight him, but then–" Green flames exploded before them and Xitou ducked down.

"What's going on?"

Xitou looked back to find Reitrin approaching. She looked awful in blood and dirt smudged clothes and her hair unevenly cut. Xitou turned his back to her before she could recognize him.

"Take cover, Ms. Nichol," said Hiro sharply. "I know you've come to like danger, but this is no place for you."

Reitrin covered her head with her arms to keep the falling ashes from getting in her hair. She was bewildered until she looked past him and saw Etakai struggling to stand up in the midst of the flames that were now mostly green and still spreading.

The fire snapped like snakes and coiled around Etakai as if longing to devour him with everything else.

Reitrin gasped. "Etakai? What is he doing?"

Her question was answered when Etakai hurled green flames at them.

Reitrin stared with disbelief and did not move out of the way in time. Hiro stepped in front of her and took the force of the flames head-on.

"Hiro!" Reitrin cried in alarm.

Hiro cursed and beat the flames off his suit. His shirt and body armor was ruined. It hung off him like slime. He tossed it aside, revealing his torso that was machinery from beneath his chest down.

Reitrin stared in horror. "Are you okay–"

"I'm fine. Xitou, get Reitrin out of here. Neither of you will be able to stand against Etakai when he's in this state."

"Xitou?" Reitrin caught her breath as she looked around at him. Her eyes widened. "But you–"

"There's no time for explanations," Hiro snapped. He shoved Reitrin back behind the rubble as another volley of flame rushed at them.

"I want to know what's happening," Reitrin yelled at Hiro. "Why is Etakai attacking us? And why is Xitou here?"

"Etakai is a danger to us." Hiro grabbed Reitrin's shoulders and shook her once to get her to focus. "Go with Xitou. My men have already taken your sister and Shan a safe distance away. I have to stop Etakai before it's too late."

Another volley of flames came. Reitrin pulled herself free from Hiro's grip and looked past the rubble at Etakai.

He had regained his feet and stood lopsided. The fang tattoo beneath his green eye had lengthened so far that both points had crossed on his cheek and were creeping down towards his jaw. Black ink spilled from the corner of his mouth and the three wounds in his chest were spurting black ink as well.

Reitrin had never seen anything like it. Her stomach turned and when Xitou took her arm to lead her away she could not comprehend why they thought she had to escape.

"He needs my help," Reitrin said.

"He needs Hiro to end him, that's what he needs," said Xitou.

Reitrin's eyes widened. No. That couldn't be right. She saw more green flames fly towards them and Xitou jerked her back behind the shelter. The rubble cracked and Hiro cursed.

It wouldn't hold any longer.

"Go," he ordered.

Reitrin broke free from Xitou's grip and ran out from behind the shelter.

"No," Xitou cried, whipping back to catch her, but she slipped out of reach and ran.

"Damn her idiocy," Hiro yelled as he jumped up and chased her.

The flames licked Reitrin's skin and she winced as she charged through the fire. It smelled of ink and hurt more than she expected.

Etakai wasn't looking at her. It seemed as if he could no longer see. He was standing with his hands out and the green flames collecting on his fingertips, preparing to attack again.

"Stop it," Reitrin shouted as she reached him. The green flames shot over her head and she ducked, but then sprung up and threw her arms around Etakai's neck.

The flames roared and rose from the ground to defend Etakai. They spiraled around Reitrin as if trying to pull her off, but she buried her face into Etakai's shoulder and held on as if her life depended on it.

"Etakai, knock it off," she said. "Hiro and Xitou are in danger–" She screamed when the flames cut across her face. She buried her face deeper into Etakai's shoulder. "Why are you doing this? After all I went through to bring you back, why are you attacking us?"

"Get away from him, Reitrin," Hiro shouted from somewhere beyond the flames.

"Etakai, I don't want them to hurt you," Reitrin whispered into his shoulder. "And I don't want you to be like this. You're my friend. If that means anything to you then stop this."

The heat ebbed.

Reitrin lifted her head.

The green flames were dying down.

She stared at Etakai's face and found both his eyes were blue and the tattoo was shrinking back to its normal length, leaving a bleeding cut behind that bled red blood instead of black.

Etakai blinked and looked down at Reitrin as if in a daze.

"Are you okay?" Reitrin felt tears filling her eyes and Etakai gave her a confused face.

"Where … Fevros?" He spoke, but blood slipped from his lips and dripped down his chin.

"I'm sure he's long gone," Reitrin told him. "Are you okay?"

Etakai was quiet for a moment, but then he shook his head. "No." He lifted his hand and touched one of the holes in his chest. He looked down at them and Reitrin stepped back.

"Eta–" she began, but Etakai collapsed into her arms. His weight made Reitrin crash to her knees and she yelled in pain.

"You idiot," Hiro shouted as he and Xitou ran to her. "What did you hope to accomplish by running into danger like that?"

"This, I guess?" Reitrin looked up at him with tears rolling down her face. "Hiro, I don't know what's going on. Why did Etakai attack everyone? He said he was a hero in his storybook. Was that a lie?"

"I don't know," said Hiro as he knelt beside her and checked Etakai's wounds. "But you can tell the writer who created him wanted him to suffer. Look, the green flames were burning him too."

All along Etakai's arms and face were spiraling burns. The same burn patterns were on Reitrin also and she winced when she realized how much they hurt.

"I pity him," said Hiro grimly. "It would have been better for him to die from his wounds than almost kill his only friend."

Reitrin bowed her head and let her tears fall.

Chapter Twenty-Seven
Temporary Peace

The explosion and flames could not be overlooked by the fire department. They were at the scene only minutes after Hiro and Xitou took Etakai and Reitrin away. There were many who passed by to look at the damage since the explosions could be heard across the city.

Sia, who had been removed from the fight along with Shan by two members of the Secret Police, was one who looked at the damage.

She saw the fire turned from green to orange and she smelled the stench of burning ink in the air. That was before Shan came and told her Hiro had taken Etakai and Reitrin into the apartment.

The two of them hurried to Reitrin's apartment. They were heavily bruised from the explosion so they could not go too fast.

One of the members of the Secret Police stood just inside the building armed with a rifle and guarding the entrance of the basement. He nodded to Sia and Shan and opened the door for them.

They peeked down the dark staircase before making their way down into the laundry room below.

Inside, there were blankets laid out and candles burning to light the area.

As soon as Sia's feet touched the basement floor she was locked in the direct stare of Hiro.

"No stupid questions," he said before turning away. He was kneeling beside the pile of blankets with bandages, ointment, and thread. On the blankets was Etakai.

Reitrin was sitting with her back against the far wall. She had burns on her skin and a distant expression. Her gaze did not shift from Etakai once.

Sia went to Reitrin and sat on the floor beside her and Shan sat on her other side. They were silent as they watched Hiro tend to Etakai's injuries. Sia had seen everything that happened, even after the officers from the Secret Police took her and Shan far away so they would not get hurt.

"Well," she murmured after a long silence. "At least you guys got rid of the clouds."

Reitrin nodded. She glanced at Sia, then at Shan who was cleaning his glasses on his sleeve.

"Hiro and I found the device," murmured Reitrin as she looked back at Hiro. She was silent for a while longer, but then glanced at her sister. "Are you both alright?"

"Yeah, just a little bruised from the explosion and rattled from the chaos," replied Sia.

The door upstairs opened and Xitou came down with a bundle of clothes under his arm. He saw Reitrin and paused, but then nodded to her and went to Hiro, placing the clothes beside him.

"Glen brought these for you."

"Thanks," said Hiro. He looked at the second set of clothes under Xitou's arm. "And are those for Etakai?"

"With how much weight he lost in the history book, I doubt they'll fit him," replied Xitou. Etakai looked frail beneath the burns and bandages.

"They'll do for now," replied Hiro. "Send word

to the others. Let them know all that has happened. We will need more guards around this building, inside and out. We don't know what Fevros will do next."

"Yes, sir," replied Xitou. He set the second bundle of clothes aside and then left the basement.

"What's going to happen to Etakai?" Reitrin directed the question to Hiro.

"We will be keeping him under strict surveillance from now on," replied Hiro as he finished the stitches and began to bandage the wound. "We've suspected the possibility of him turning on you, but we did not realize it would be caused by Fevros."

Reitrin bowed her head. Xitou had told her and Hiro everything he had seen and done before they arrived at the scene. They knew about Fevros and the light blue fire. It was Fevros who had stabbed Etakai in the chest with Etakai's own knives and Reitrin clenched her jaw when she imagined it.

"Shouldn't you both go to a doctor?" Sia whispered to Reitrin.

"The hospital need not know about their injuries," said Hiro. "I wish you had not gone there so often. Fevros has his minions watching that place all the time."

"What?" Reitrin demanded. "Why?"

"Most of the people that come out of storybooks go to the hospital or Shan's restaurant," explained Hiro.

At the mention of his name, Shan looked up. "You were watching my restaurant too?"

"Yes," replied Hiro. He cut the last thread of Etakai's stitches and began to bandage him. "Your restaurant, the hospital, the library, and this apartment are places we have witnessed book jumpers frequent."

"So you already knew about Fevros," Reitrin guessed.

"Yes," Hiro answered. He finished bandaging Etakai and rose to his feet. He took the medical equipment with him as he went to Reitrin. He motioned for her to hold out her arms where she had the most burns.

"Thankfully Etakai didn't fry you to a crisp," muttered Hiro, setting aside his supplies and taking her arms. "These could have been a lot worse." He examined the burns then checked her face and neck. This made Sia shoot Reitrin a look of envy.

She hated that her sister had been hurt, but part of her wished she had been hurt too so the handsome officer would give her attention too.

"Will Etakai be okay?" Reitrin asked as Hiro drew back and opened the jar of salve.

"Eventually," replied Hiro as he smeared salve over Reitrin's burns. "I will ask you to keep an eye on him. I'm sure you're the only person he will trust right now and for the time being we cannot leave him to himself. Not after all he has gone through."

Reitrin frowned, but then bowed her head to watch Hiro wrap up her arms. Her neck was also wrapped up and Hiro placed bandages on her face.

When he finished he stepped back and looked at Etakai. The man was still out cold.

Hiro sighed and packed up the medical supplies. "You all need to sleep. It's late and you've been through a lot."

"Where do you suggest we stay?" Sia asked

bitterly. "In this cold basement?"

"For tonight, yes," replied Hiro. "Tomorrow I will tend to relocation details for each of you. However, you should all be grateful. You'll wake up to a real sunrise." He left the supplies on the floor beside Reitrin. "I'll check in later." He then left the basement, taking the steps two at a time.

The door to the basement shut and Reitrin sighed.

"Sia, do you have the strength to make up beds for you and Shan?" Reitrin asked as she stood up.

"I could find somewhere else to sleep," said Sia quickly. "You need to sleep more than…" Her words faded when Reitrin walked to Etakai and sat down beside him. She looked grim.

Sia frowned. "Well, okay," she muttered.

"I'll help," said Shan, though it pained him to stand. The two of them gathered blankets out of the storage cabinets and made beds for themselves away from Etakai and Reitrin.

Sia looked back at her sister. She was not moving from Etakai's side. Sia glanced at Shan who frowned and shook his head. They both knew leaving Reitrin alone was best. The two of them slid under the covers and, though the floor was hard and uncomfortable, they were too exhausted to complain and fell asleep at once.

The silence of the basement dragged on. The candles illuminating the stone walls snapped from time to time, but Reitrin did not jump. She stayed by Etakai, watching him with her arms wrapped around her legs.

Etakai's breath was faint, but Hiro said he was stable. The fang tattoo was back to normal, but there were pale lines where it had cut him. They healed fast.

"Why did this happen to you?" Reitrin whispered. Her voice sounded loud in the dark basement. "And why did I decide to make you my friend?" She checked the pulse on his wrist, gazing at his face. His expression was one of pain and Reitrin wished she could do something to ease his suffering.

She sighed and lay down on the floor beside him. "Heal quickly. We have to figure out what's going on." She shut her eyes, dozing off into an uneasy slumber.

Etakai opened his eyes partially and looked at her. She had fallen asleep holding onto his wrist. Etakai narrowed his eyes and watched her sadly.

She had risked her life for him twice now, something no one had ever done for him before.

Etakai did not remove his wrist from her grip. "We're even now." He shut his eyes. "Thank you, Reitrin."

Reitrin sighed and Etakai felt her relax a little more. She was asleep, but he knew she had heard his words.

Etakai smiled and then fell asleep again.

*   *   *

It was later that night when Reitrin woke up. She was cold, but that wasn't what had woken her. She had become aware of a presence in the room. She lifted her head, hoping it was just her imagination.

"I need that wrap back," said Aoiro, standing over her with his arms crossed. His red hair looked dark in the shadows of night. "I know it's comfortable, but it's also valuable and I can't have it fall into the wrong hands."

Reitrin watched Aoiro, but then carefully stood up and faced him. "You told me not to remove it without you nearby. Why?"

"Just in case," replied Aoiro. "A lot could go wrong."

"If you're evil then wouldn't you want something to go wrong?"

"Wrap, please." Aoiro motioned with his hand impatiently.

Reitrin lifted her shirt to show the wrap she had been wearing for months. It looked as if it had not been worn for longer than a few minutes though. "What could go wrong?" Reitrin glanced at Aoiro.

"If your wound was fatal to begin with you could bleed out and die," replied Aoiro. "But I need the wrap back right now, so hopefully that won't happen."

Reitrin stared at him, then at the wrap. "Why didn't you tell me that to begin with?"

"Would you have still used it and gone after Etakai?" Aoiro arched an eyebrow at her and Reitrin gave him a sharp look.

"Yes," she replied.

"So, these are the consequences for your valor," replied Aoiro. "Give me back the wrap, please."

Reitrin knew she wouldn't get away with any more delays. She unstrapped the wrap at her side, but hesitated. A tingling sensation had gone through her abdominal and she felt cold fear wash over her. It was her wound. She looked quickly at Aoiro who tapped his wrist, showing her she was wasting time. Reitrin looked down, but then shut her eyes and peeled off the wrap.

The tingling sensation grew stronger and she felt Aoiro step towards her.

"I guess you'll be okay." He took the wrap from her hands. "Looks like someone gave you some healing herbs before you put the wrap on."

Reitrin opened her eyes and looked up just as Aoiro vanished in a burst of light. She stared at where he had been, but then looked down at her stomach.

There was a scar of light pink skin where Flamelord's sword had stabbed her.

Reitrin passed her fingers over the scar. It was soft as silk and she took her hand away as if it had burned her. It was healed. She reached to her back and felt for any blood.

It was clean. She felt the same soft scar and lowered her hand.

"I wonder who gave me healing herbs," she whispered as she rolled her shirt back down. "I can't think of anyone who would." Reitrin sighed and looked down at Etakai. He seemed peaceful now and it brought a small smile to Reitrin's face.

For the time being, everything was okay.

To Be Continued